LONG TABI BOOTS

rubber soles for excellent grip. Black cotton uppers
nd up close to the knee. Also available in ankle-high style.

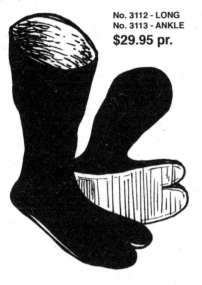

No. 3112 - LONG
No. 3113 - ANKLE
$29.95 pr.

SAI

Stainless steel with leather wrapped handguards.

As seen in *Elektra: Assassin!*

Available in 3 popular lengths.

No. 1895 - 18" long
No. 1896 - 19 1/2" long
No. 1897 - 21 1/2" long
$24.95 pr.

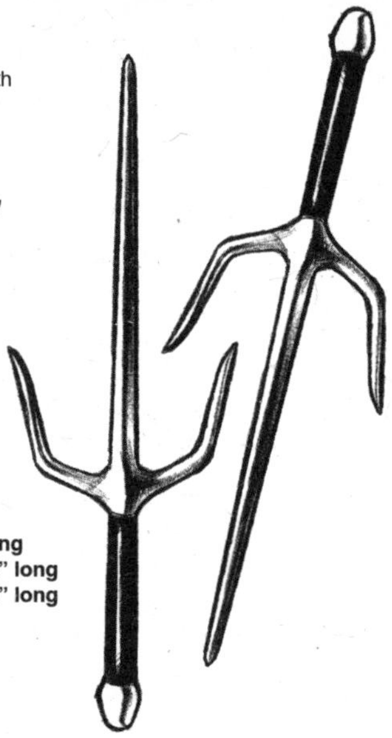

TRADITI

Nylon stri

No. 1850 - $...

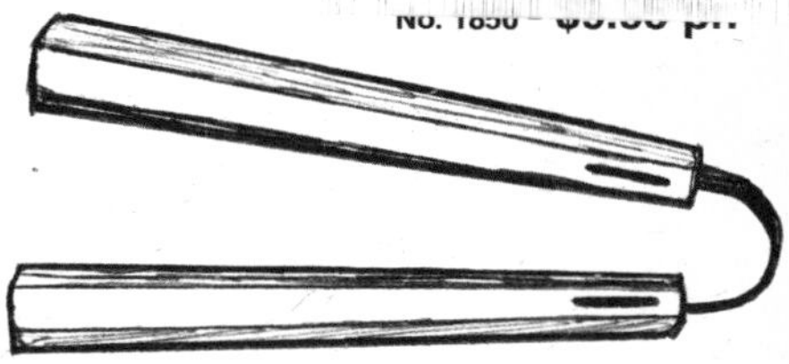

NINJUK

Speed grip black hardwood, ball-bearing swivel, steel cap and chain.

No. 1750 - $19.95 pr.

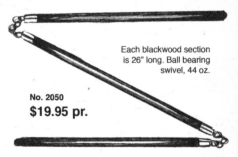

TABI TUBE SOCKS

t toe design. Dry-Fit socks maintain a perfect balance
omfort and durability. Cotton polyester blend and spandex,
sock will give you a better fit that won't lose its shape.
roved ventilation and breathability allow your feet to stay
and dry throughout your secret ninja mission.

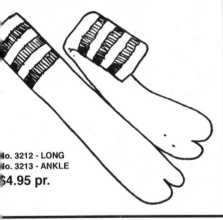

lo. 3212 - LONG
lo. 3213 - ANKLE
$4.95 pr.

BLACK NINJA OUTFIT

Constructed of a poly/cotton, wash n' wear fabric for easy care.

ADULT SIZES - Available in size 3, 4, 5, and 6 only. Traditional styling includes head wrap, hidden pocket for stars, drawstring waist, pants tie-downs and a hand/forearm sleeve.

CHILD SIZES - Available in size 000, 00, 0, 1, and 2. Traditional features in economy styling. Includes head wrap, hidden pocket for stars, drawstrings waist, pants tie-downs and a hand/forearm sleeve.

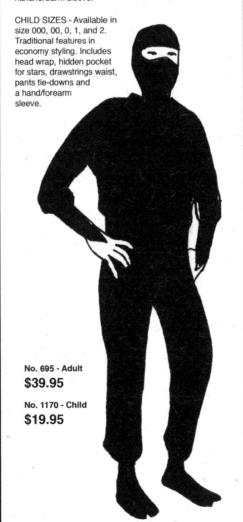

No. 695 - Adult
$39.95

No. 1170 - Child
$19.95

PRACTICE NUNCHAKU

Nylon string, foam covering.

No. 1950 - $4.95 pr.

THREE SECTIONAL STAFF

Each blackwood section is 26" long. Ball bearing swivel, 44 oz.

No. 2050
$19.95 pr.

BLACK HARDWOOD PRACTICE TONFA

Available in 2 lengths.
No. 2043 - 18" long
No. 2044 - 20" long
$19.95 pr.

NINJA BALLCAP

For those who enjoy ninjutsu and are proud of it, here's a cap you'll love for all-purpose wear. "NINJA" is boldly sillk-screened on the cap. One size fits all.

No. 2336
$9.95

NINJA

ONEY BACK GUARANTEE
you are not happy, return your purchase
ithin 30 days for a full refund.

NINJATECH

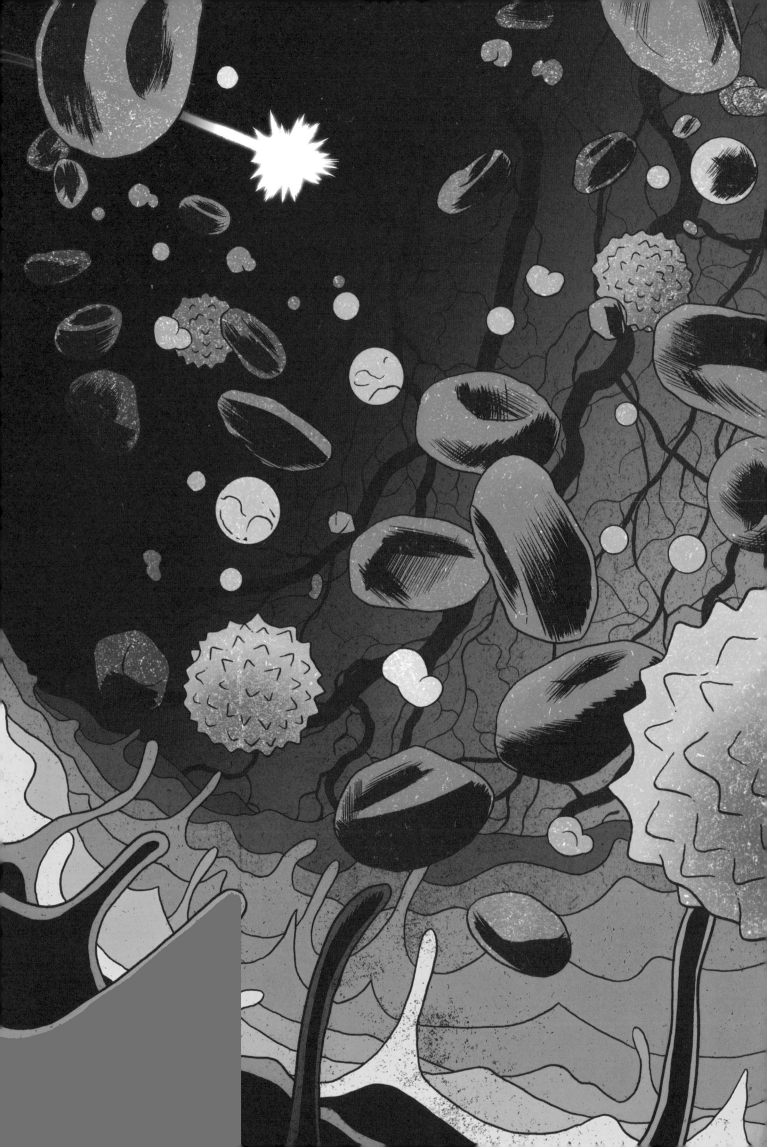

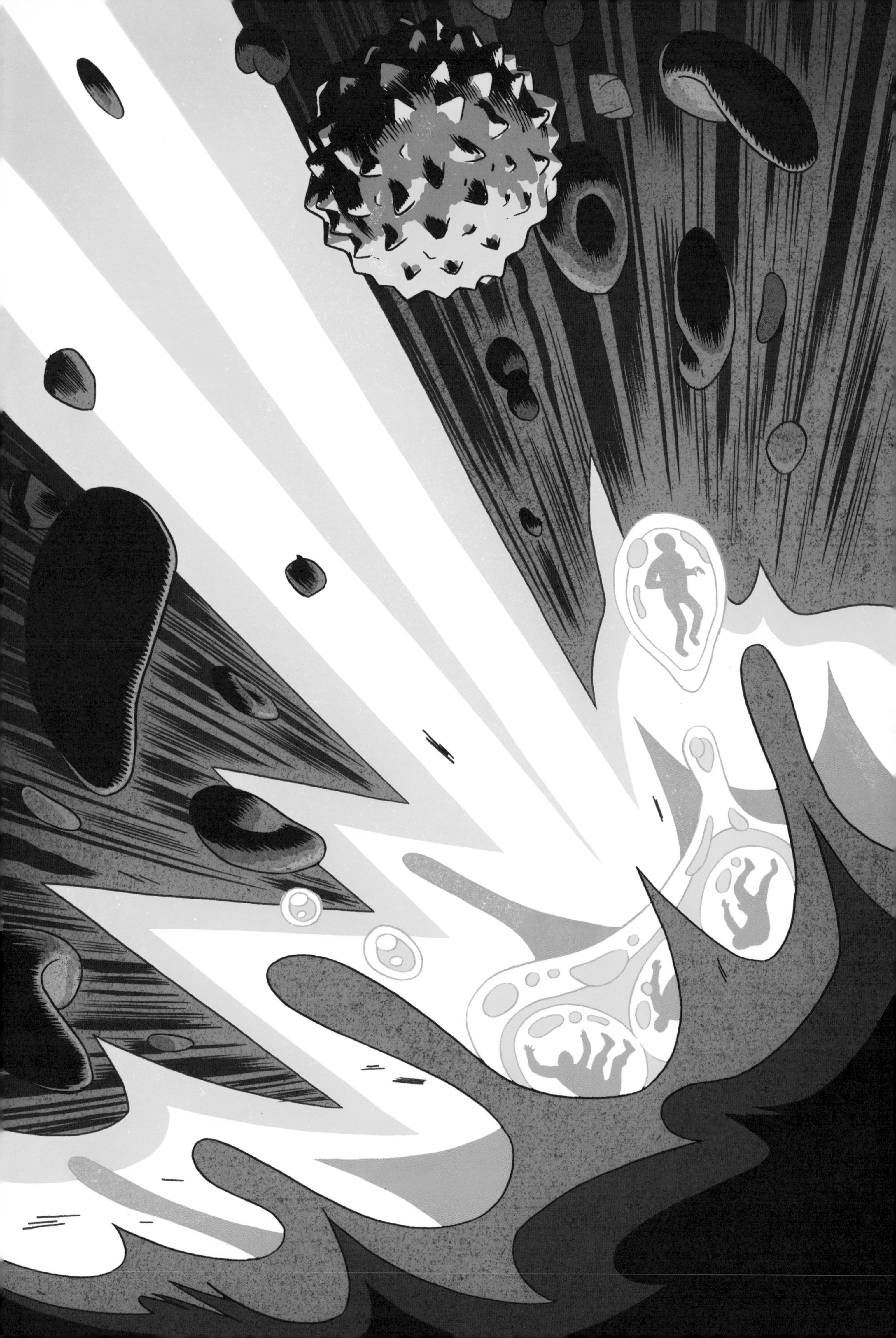

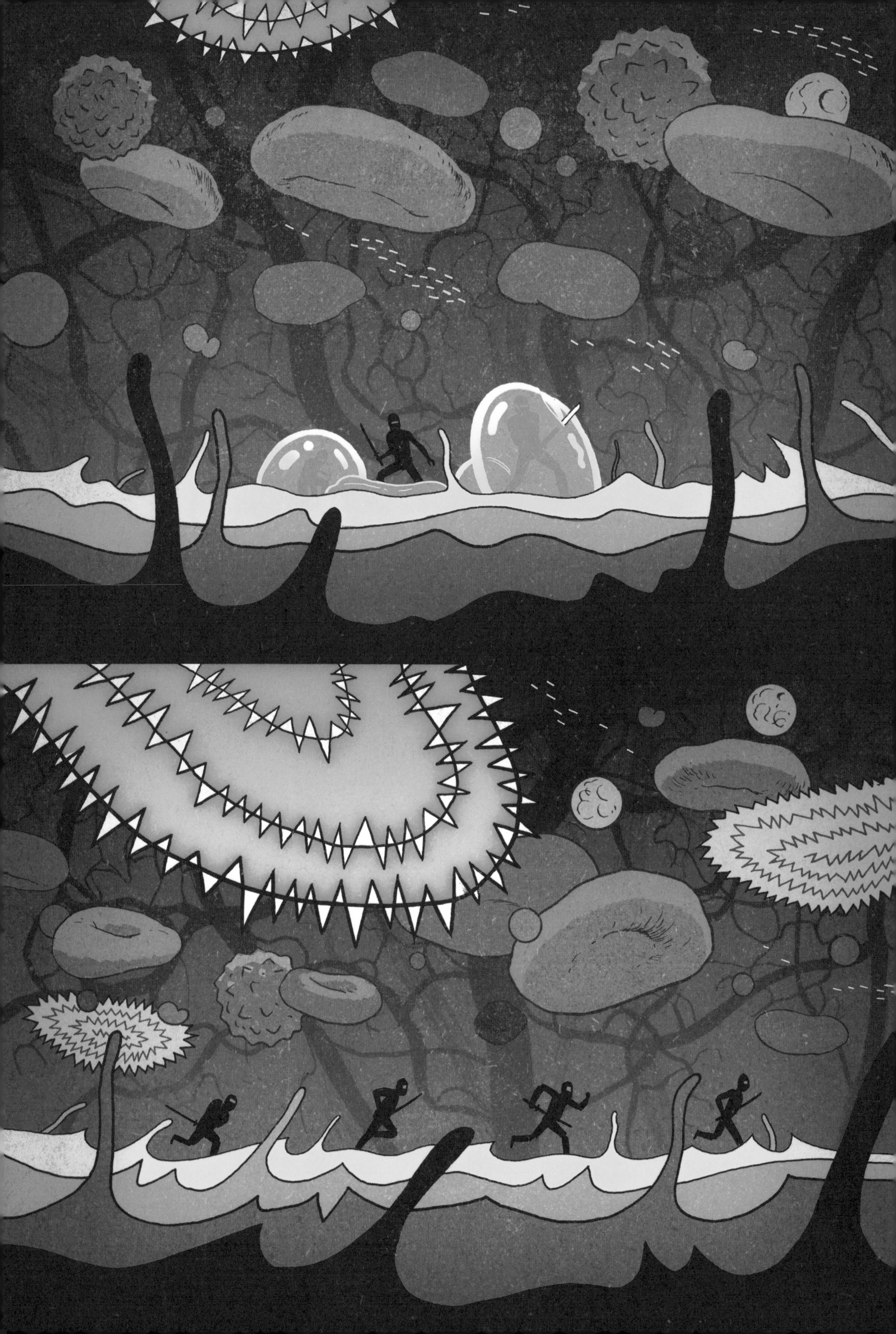

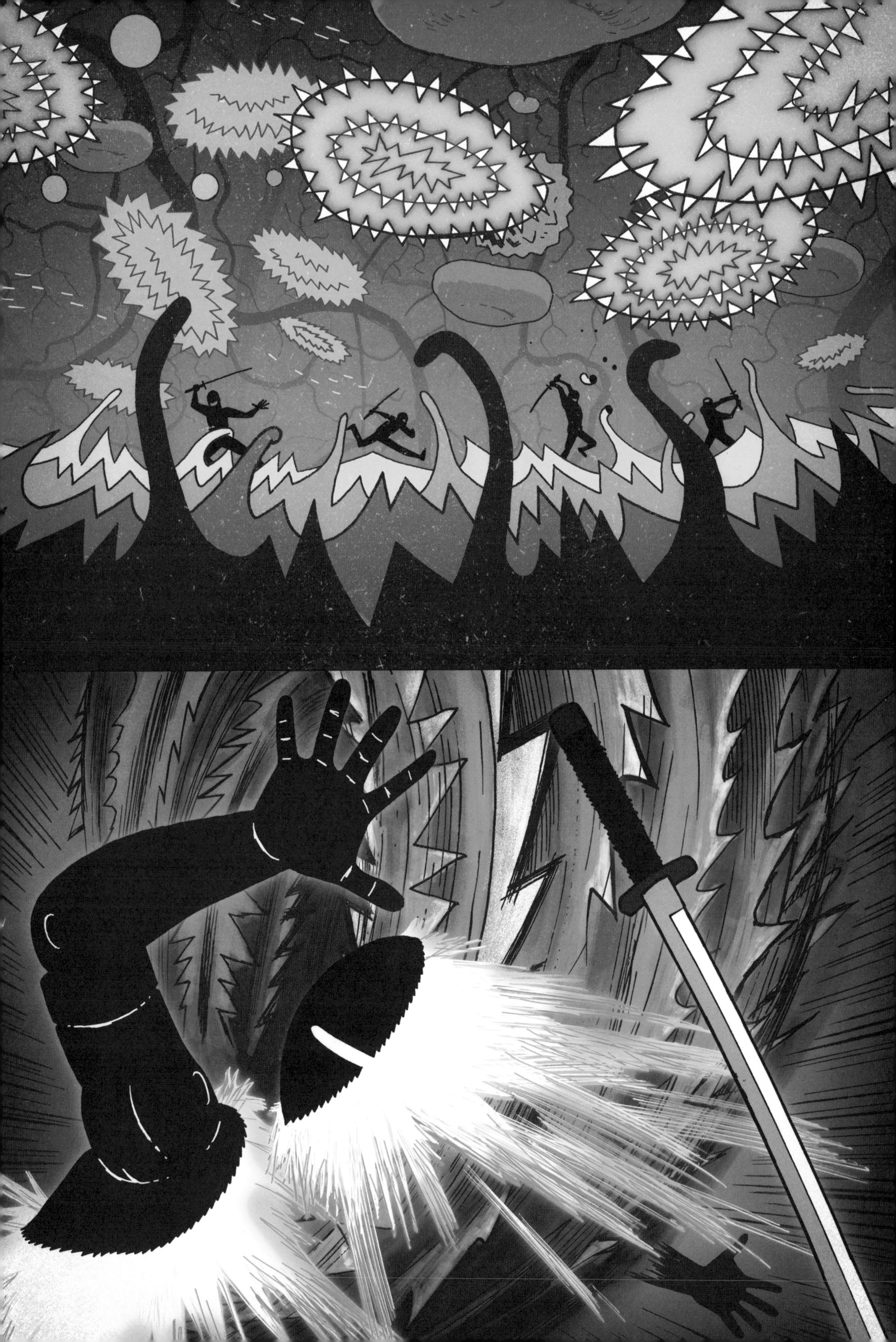

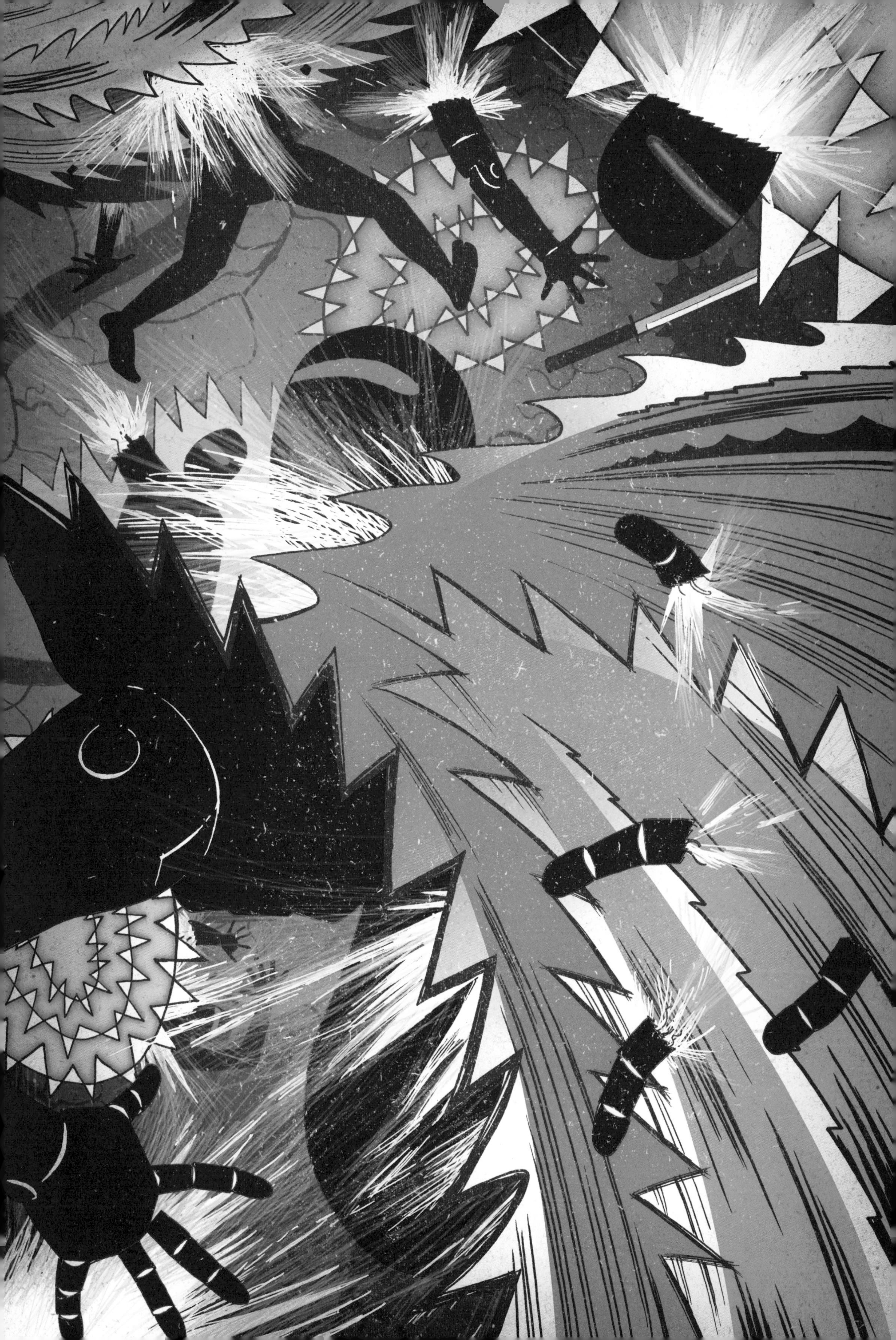

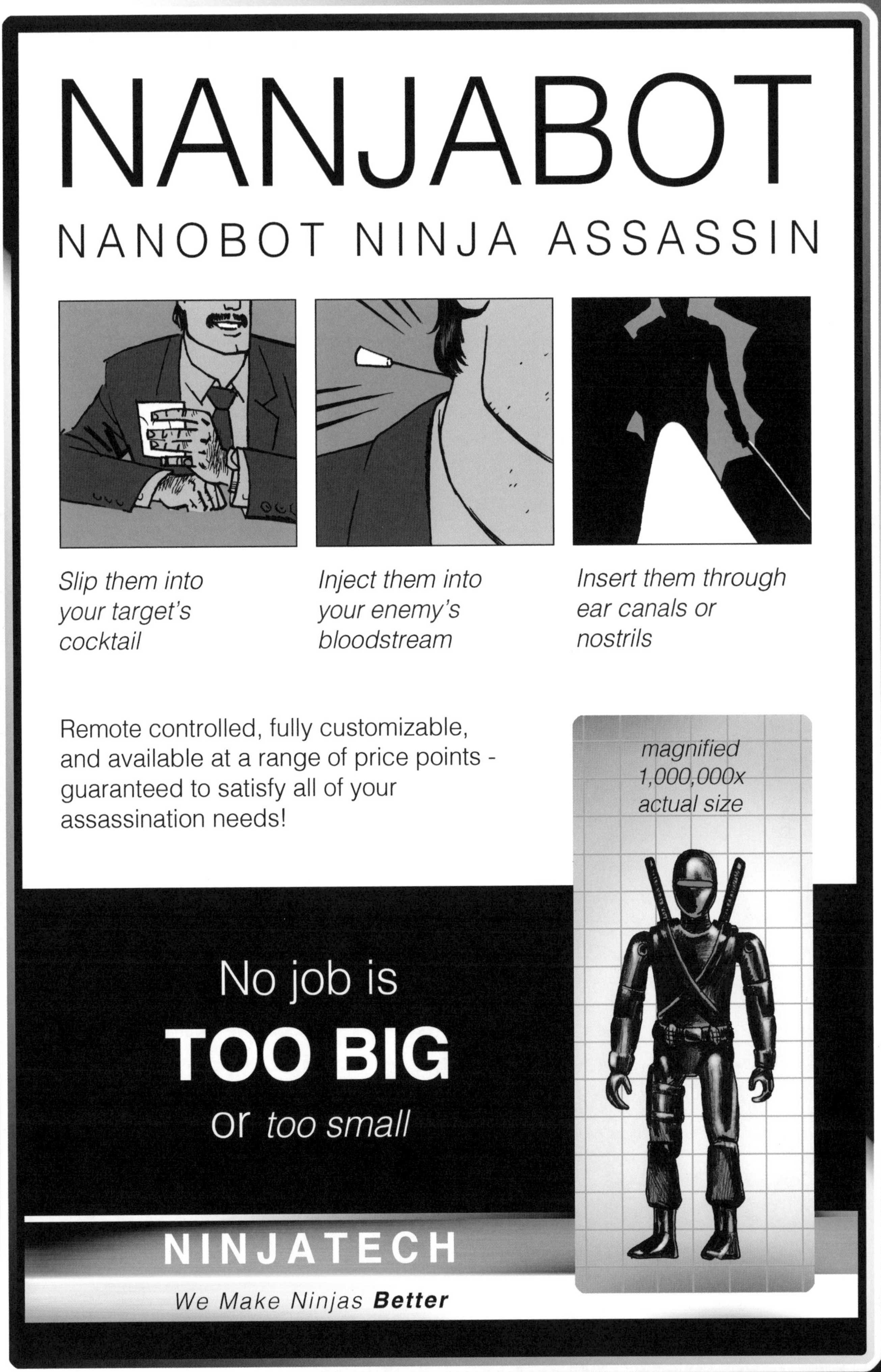
NANJABOT
NANOBOT NINJA ASSASSIN
Slip them into your target's cocktail
Inject them into your enemy's bloodstream
Insert them through ear canals or nostrils
Remote controlled, fully customizable, and available at a range of price points - guaranteed to satisfy all of your assassination needs!
magnified 1,000,000x actual size
No job is
TOO BIG
or too small
NINJATECH
We Make Ninjas Better

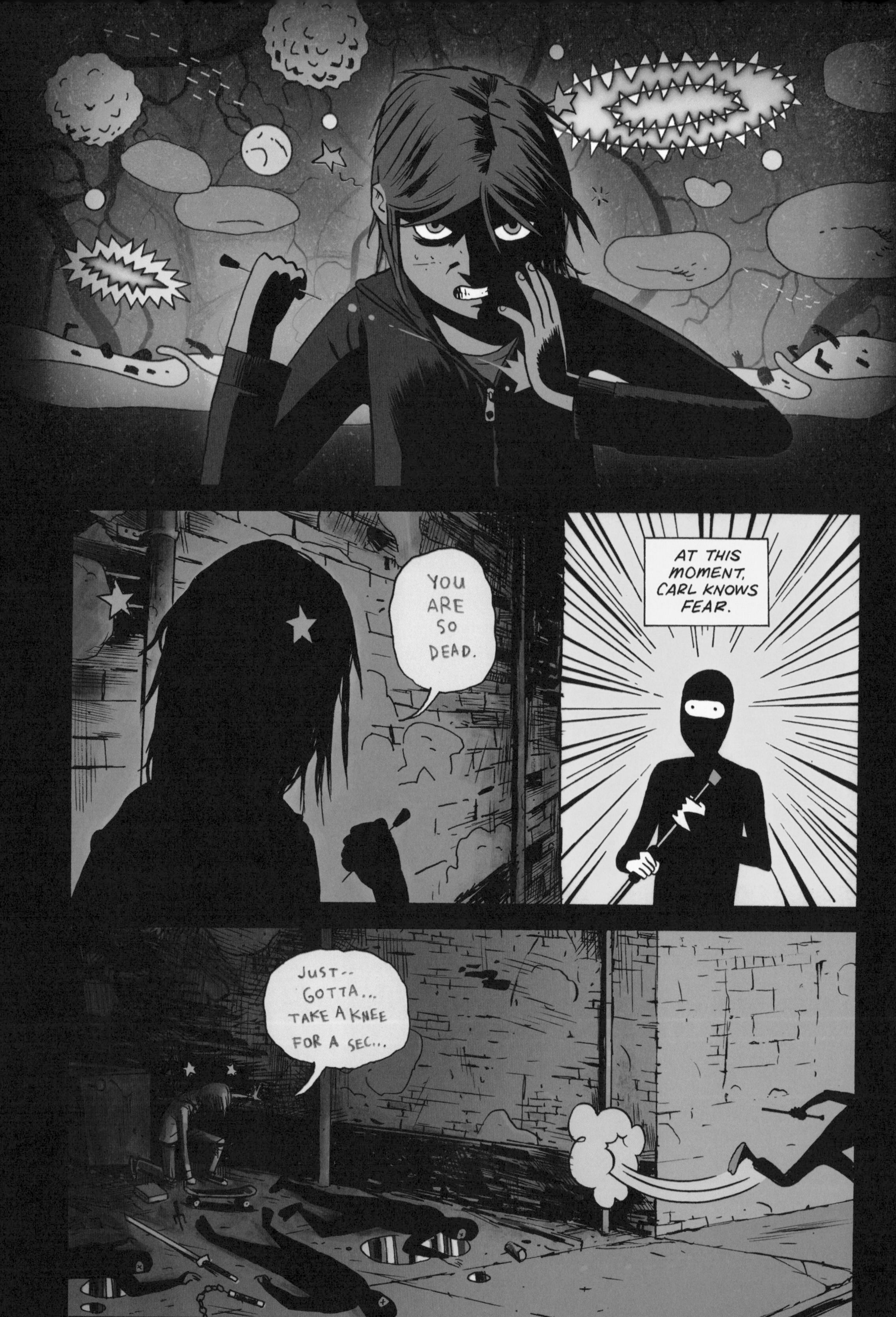
YOU ARE SO DEAD.
AT THIS MOMENT, CARL KNOWS FEAR.
JUST-- GOTTA... TAKE A KNEE FOR A SEC...

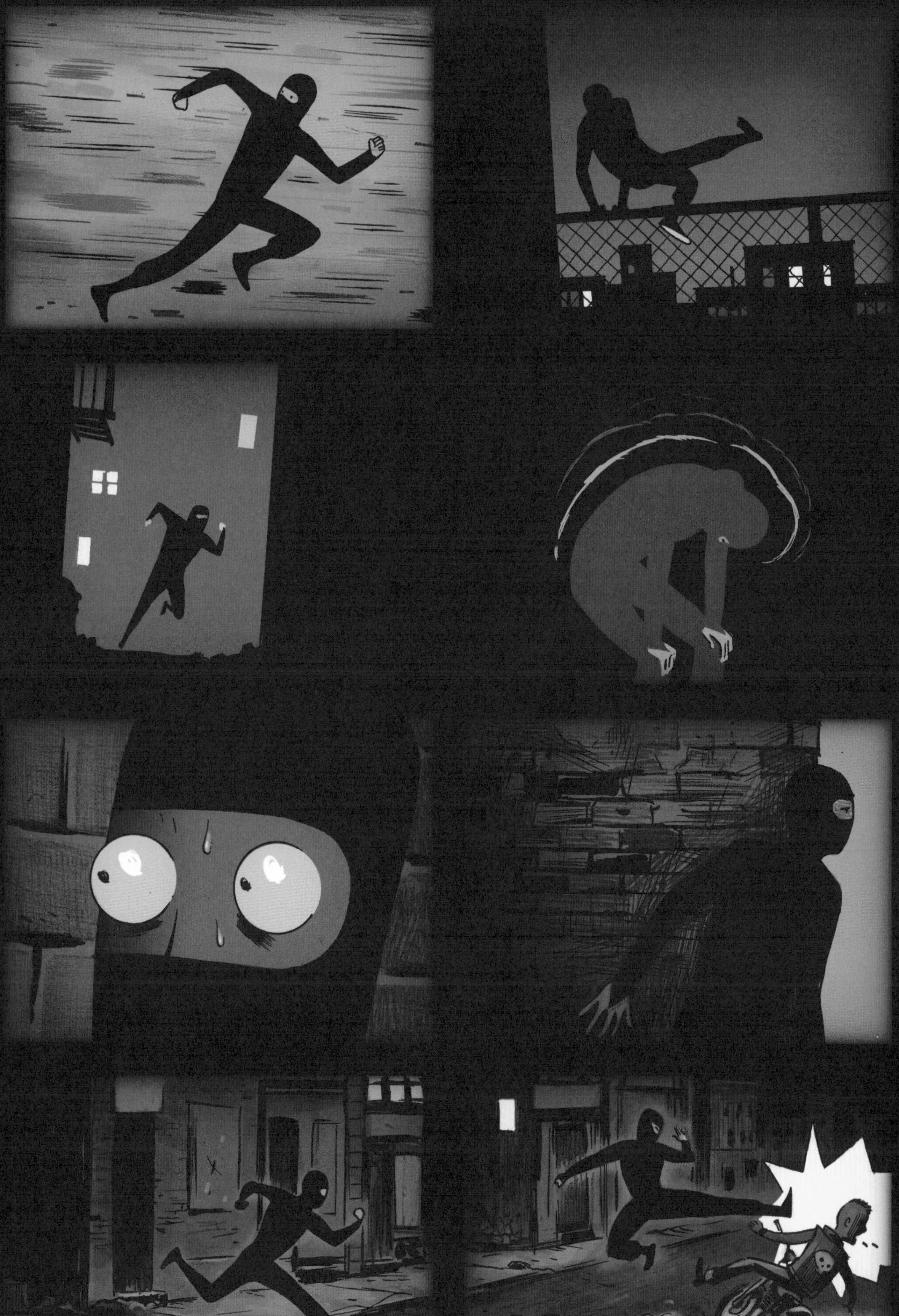

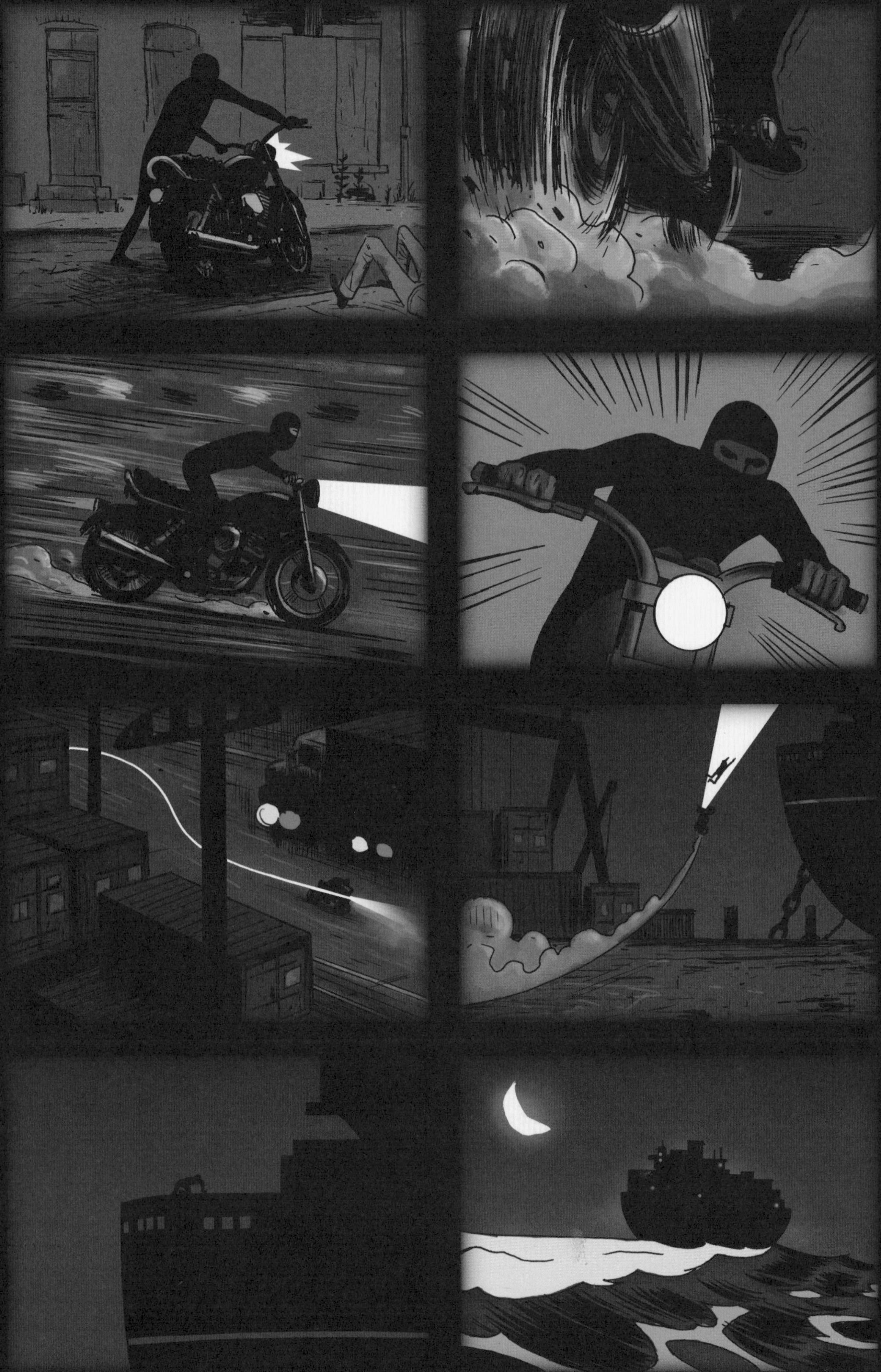

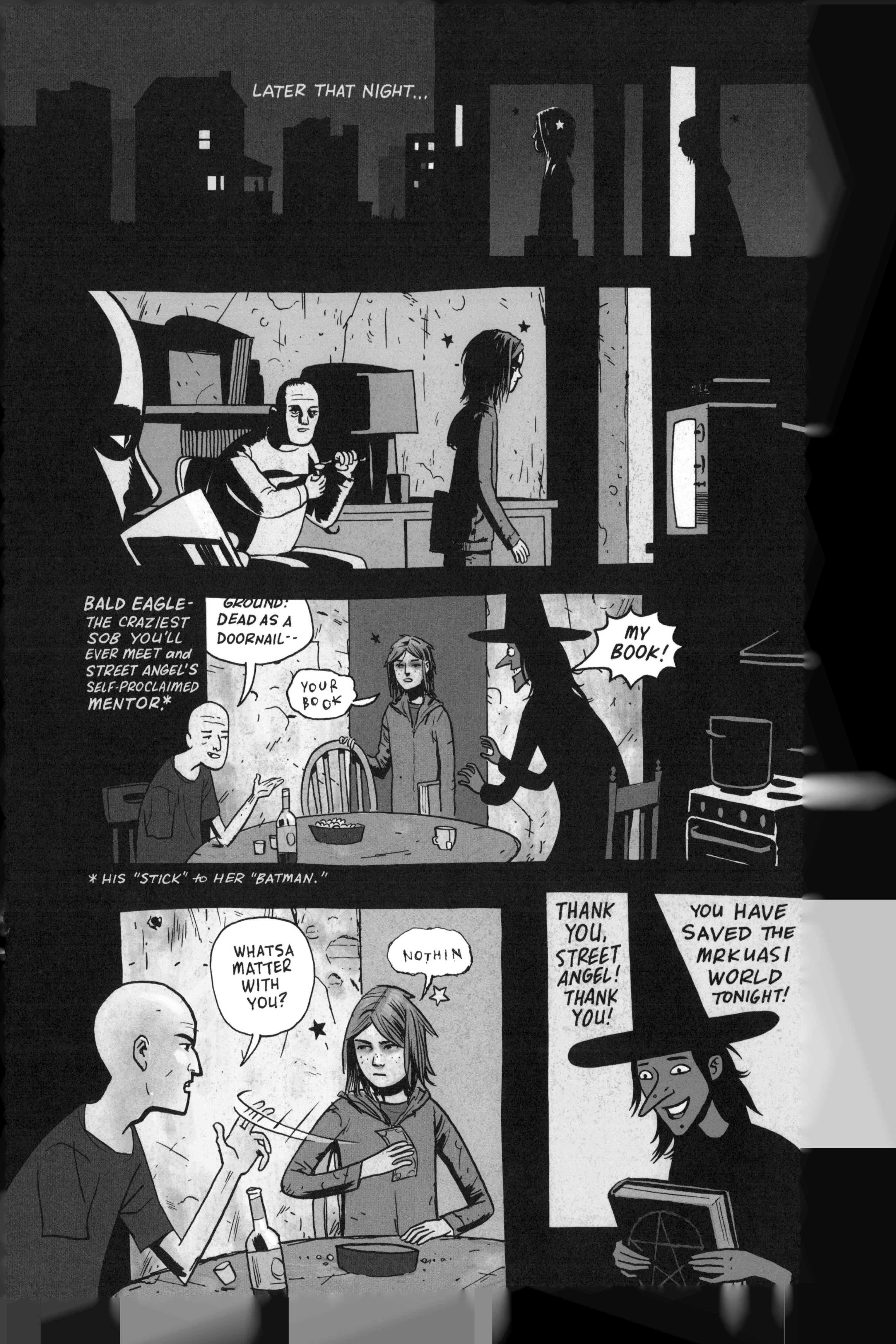
LATER THAT NIGHT...
BALD EAGLE- THE CRAZIEST SOB YOU'LL EVER MEET and STREET ANGEL'S SELF-PROCLAIMED MENTOR.*
GROUND! DEAD AS A DOORNAIL--
YOUR BOOK
MY BOOK!
* HIS "STICK" to HER "BATMAN."
WHATSA MATTER WITH YOU?
NOTHIN
THANK YOU, STREET ANGEL! THANK YOU!
YOU HAVE SAVED THE MRKUASI WORLD TONIGHT!

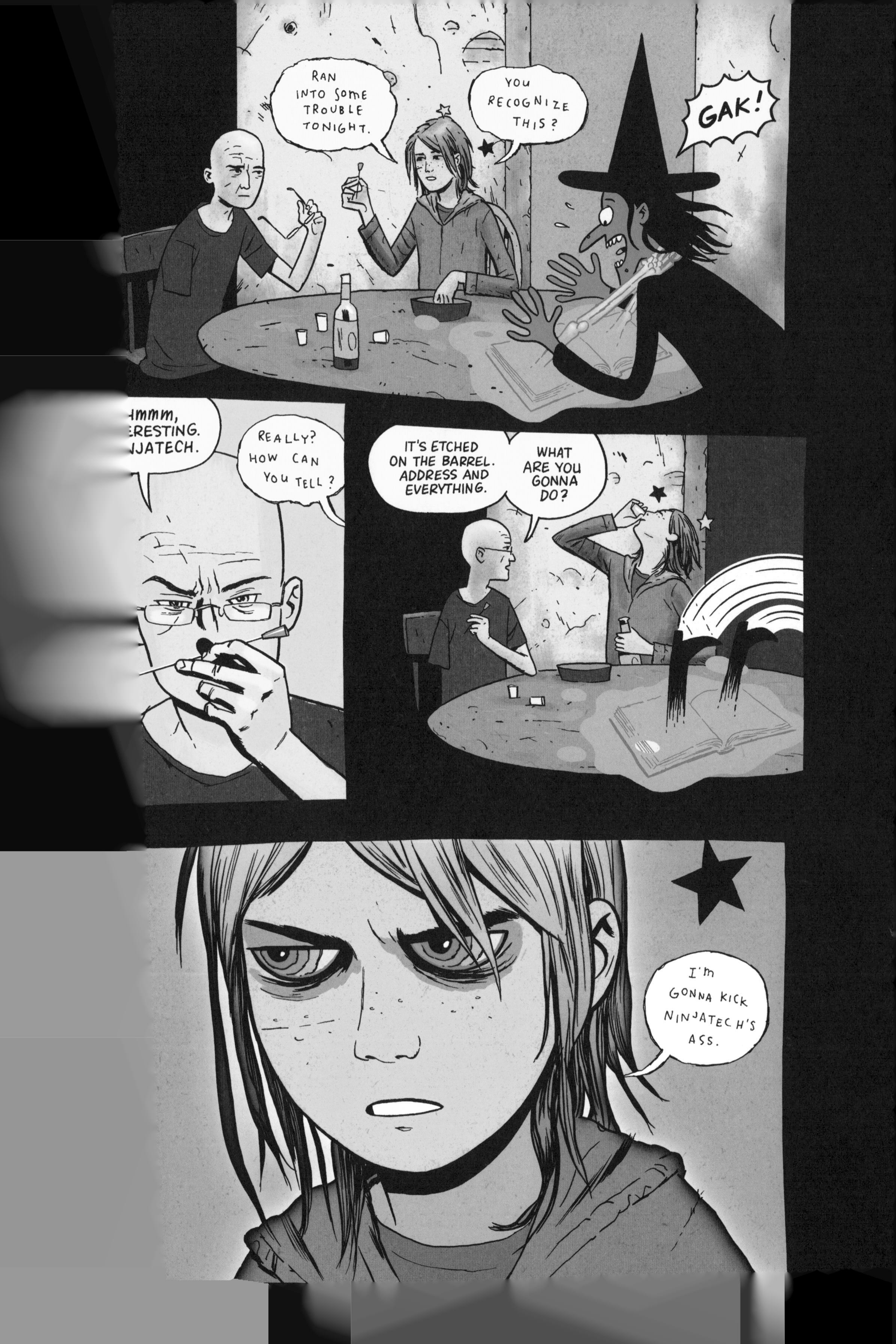
RAN INTO SOME TROUBLE TONIGHT.
YOU RECOGNIZE THIS?
GAK!
HMMM, ERESTING. NJATECH.
REALLY? HOW CAN YOU TELL?
IT'S ETCHED ON THE BARREL. ADDRESS AND EVERYTHING.
WHAT ARE YOU GONNA DO?
I'M GONNA KICK NINJATECH'S ASS.

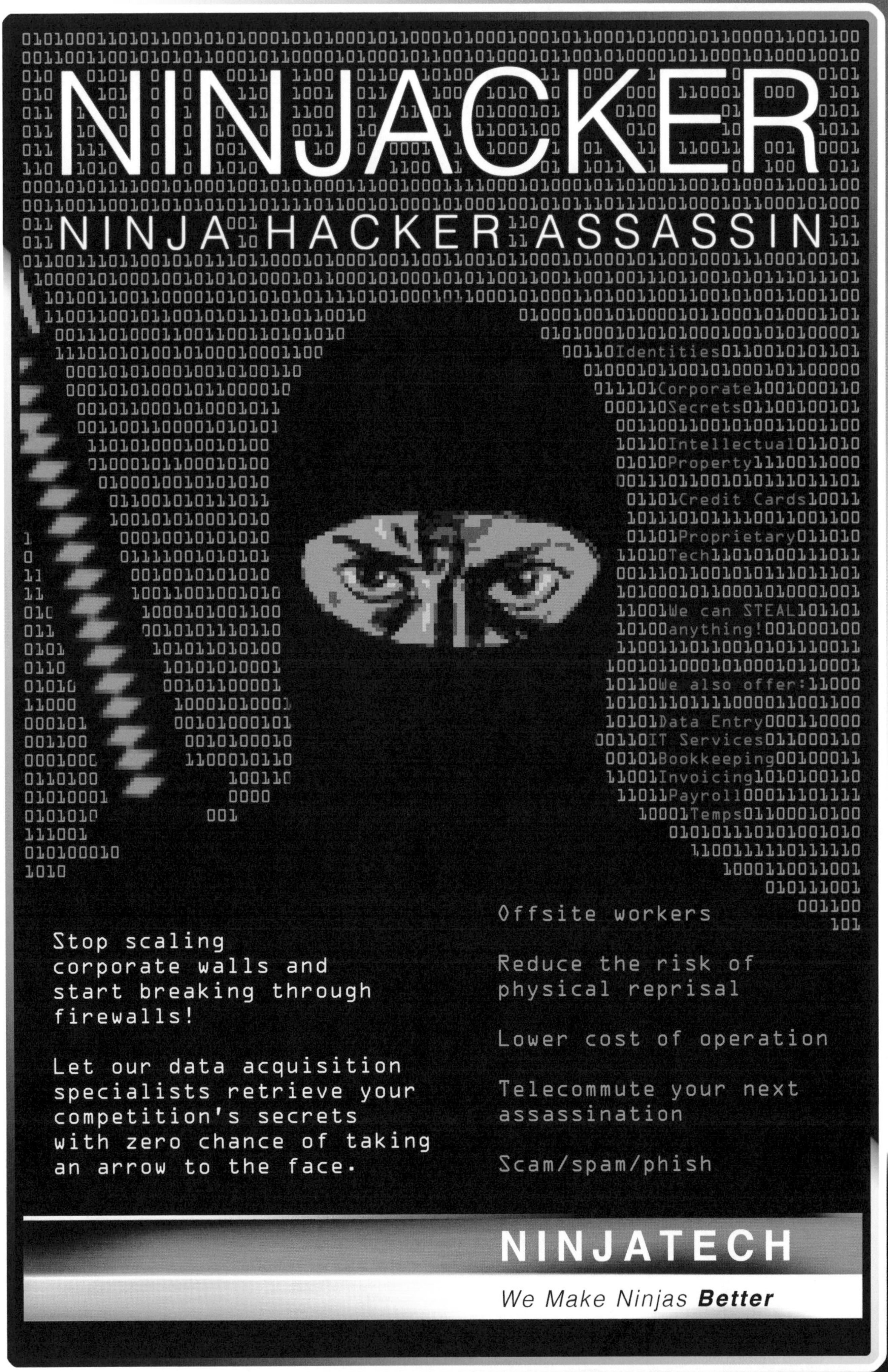
NINJACKER
NINJA HACKER ASSASSIN
Identities
Corporate Secrets
Intellectual Property
Credit Cards
Proprietary Tech
We can STEAL anything!
We also offer:
Data Entry
IT Services
Bookkeeping
Invoicing
Payroll
Temps
Stop scaling corporate walls and start breaking through firewalls!
Let our data acquisition specialists retrieve your competition's secrets with zero chance of taking an arrow to the face.
Offsite workers
Reduce the risk of physical reprisal
Lower cost of operation
Telecommute your next assassination
Scam/spam/phish
NINJATECH
We Make Ninjas Better

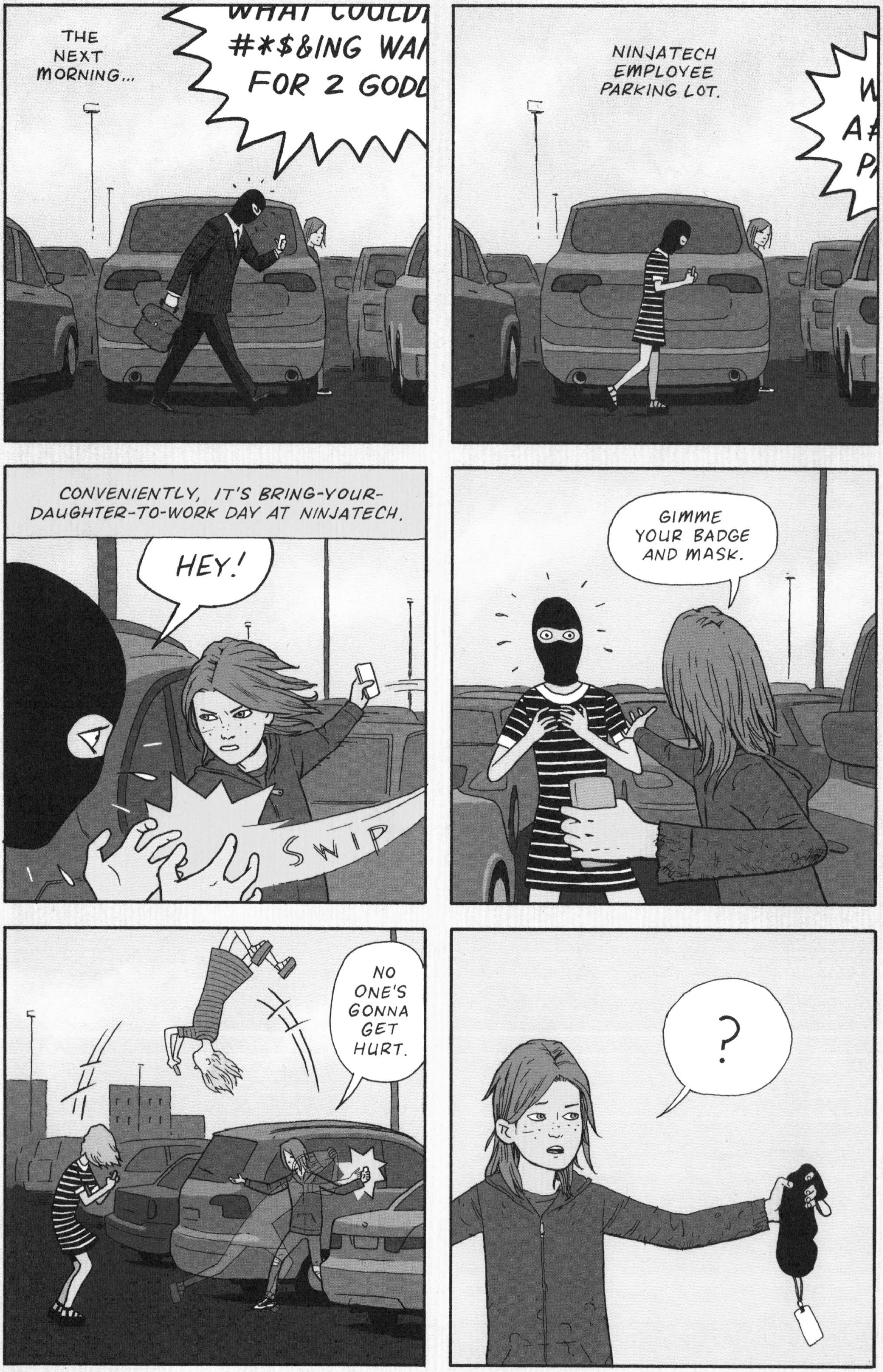
THE NEXT MORNING...
WHAT COULD
#*$&ING WA
FOR 2 GOD
NINJATECH EMPLOYEE PARKING LOT.
CONVENIENTLY, IT'S BRING-YOUR-DAUGHTER-TO-WORK DAY AT NINJATECH.
HEY!
SWIP
GIMME YOUR BADGE AND MASK.
NO ONE'S GONNA GET HURT.
?

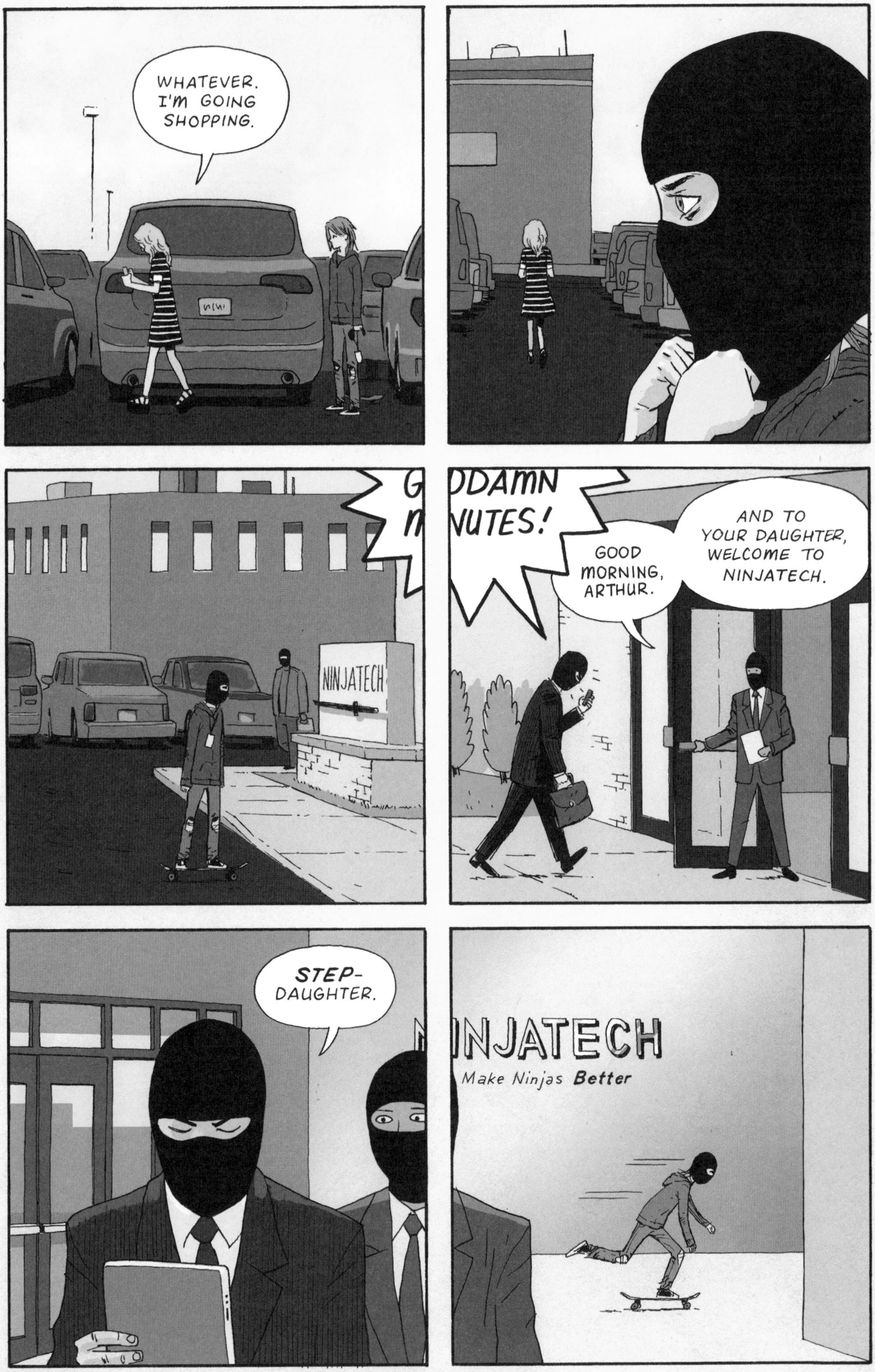
WHATEVER. I'M GOING SHOPPING.
G ODAMN
NUTES!
GOOD MORNING, ARTHUR.
AND TO YOUR DAUGHTER, WELCOME TO NINJATECH.
NINJATECH
STEP-DAUGHTER.
NINJATECH
Make Ninjas Better

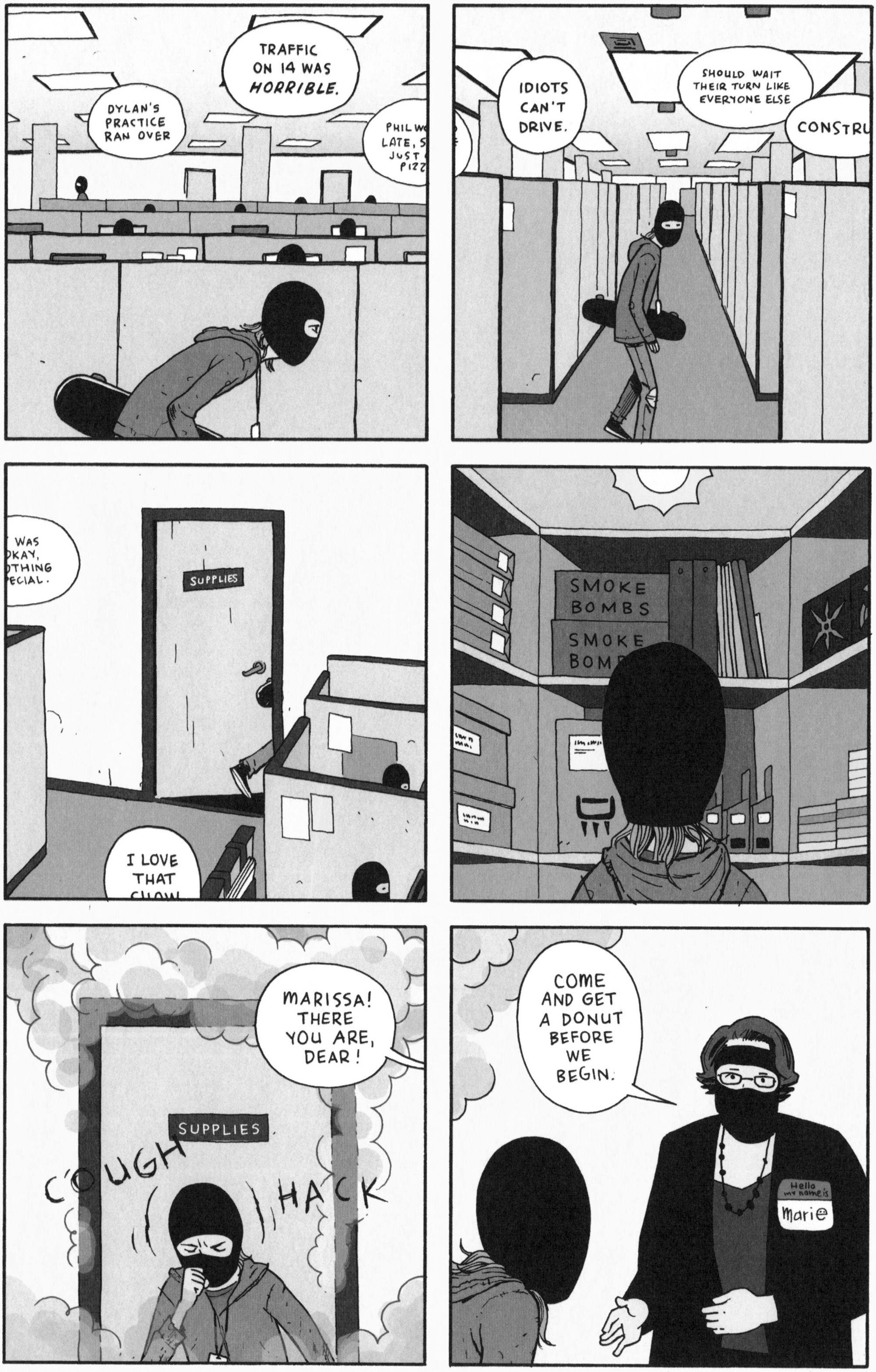

TRAFFIC ON 14 WAS HORRIBLE.
DYLAN'S PRACTICE RAN OVER
IDIOTS CAN'T DRIVE.
SHOULD WAIT THEIR TURN LIKE EVERYONE ELSE
CONSTRU
SUPPLIES
I LOVE THAT
SMOKE BOMBS
SMOKE
SUPPLIES
MARISSA! THERE YOU ARE, DEAR!
COUGH
HACK
COME AND GET A DONUT BEFORE WE BEGIN.
Hello my name is
Marie

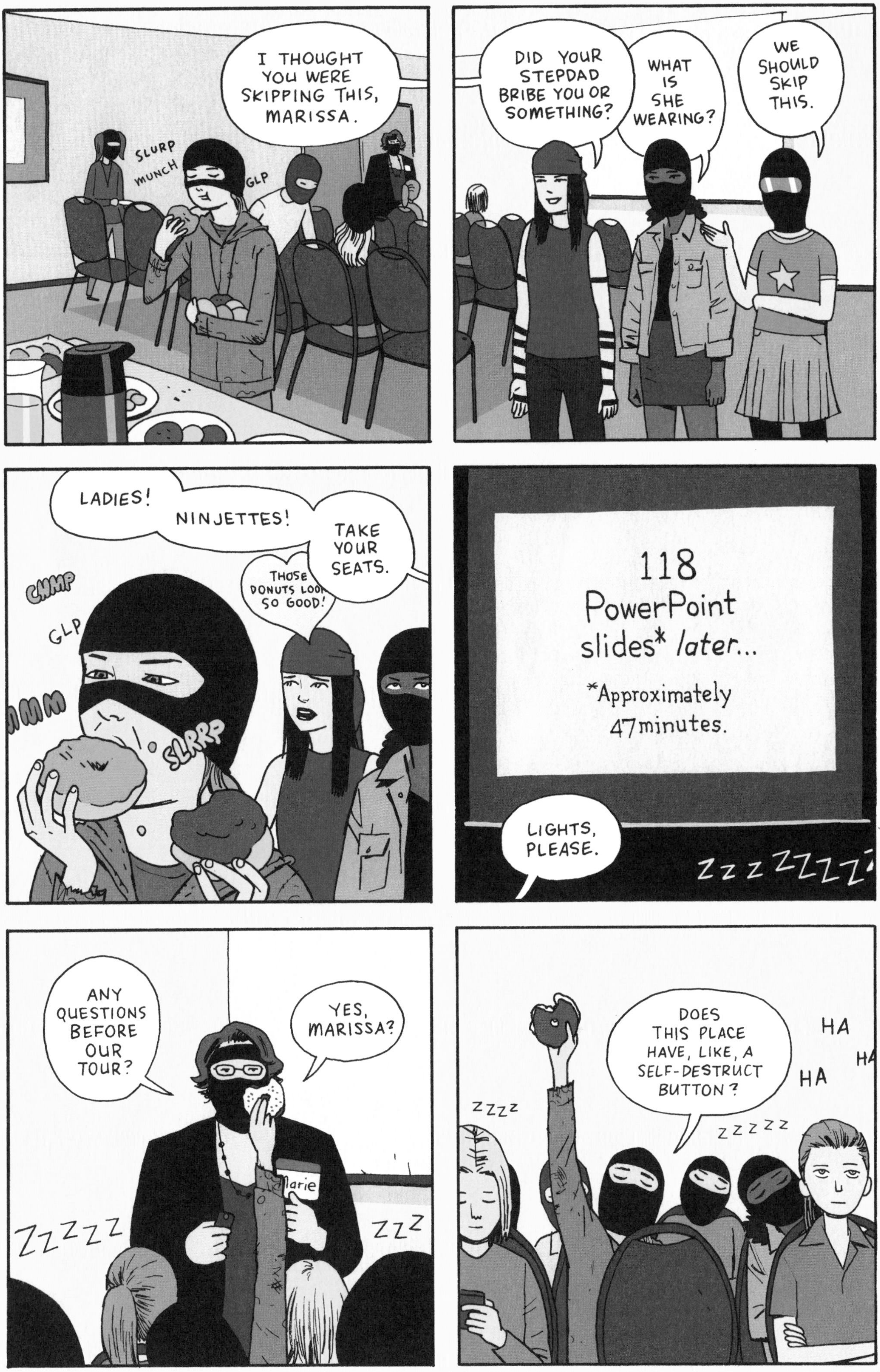
I THOUGHT YOU WERE SKIPPING THIS, MARISSA.
SLURP
MUNCH
GLP
DID YOUR STEPDAD BRIBE YOU OR SOMETHING?
WHAT IS SHE WEARING?
WE SHOULD SKIP THIS.
LADIES!
NINJETTES!
TAKE YOUR SEATS.
CHMP
GLP
MMM
SLRRP
THOSE DONUTS LOOK SO GOOD!
118 PowerPoint slides* later...
*Approximately 47minutes.
LIGHTS, PLEASE.
ZzzZZZZ
ANY QUESTIONS BEFORE OUR TOUR?
YES, MARISSA?
Marie
ZZZZZ
ZZZ
DOES THIS PLACE HAVE, LIKE, A SELF-DESTRUCT BUTTON?
HA
HA
ZZZZ
ZZZZZ

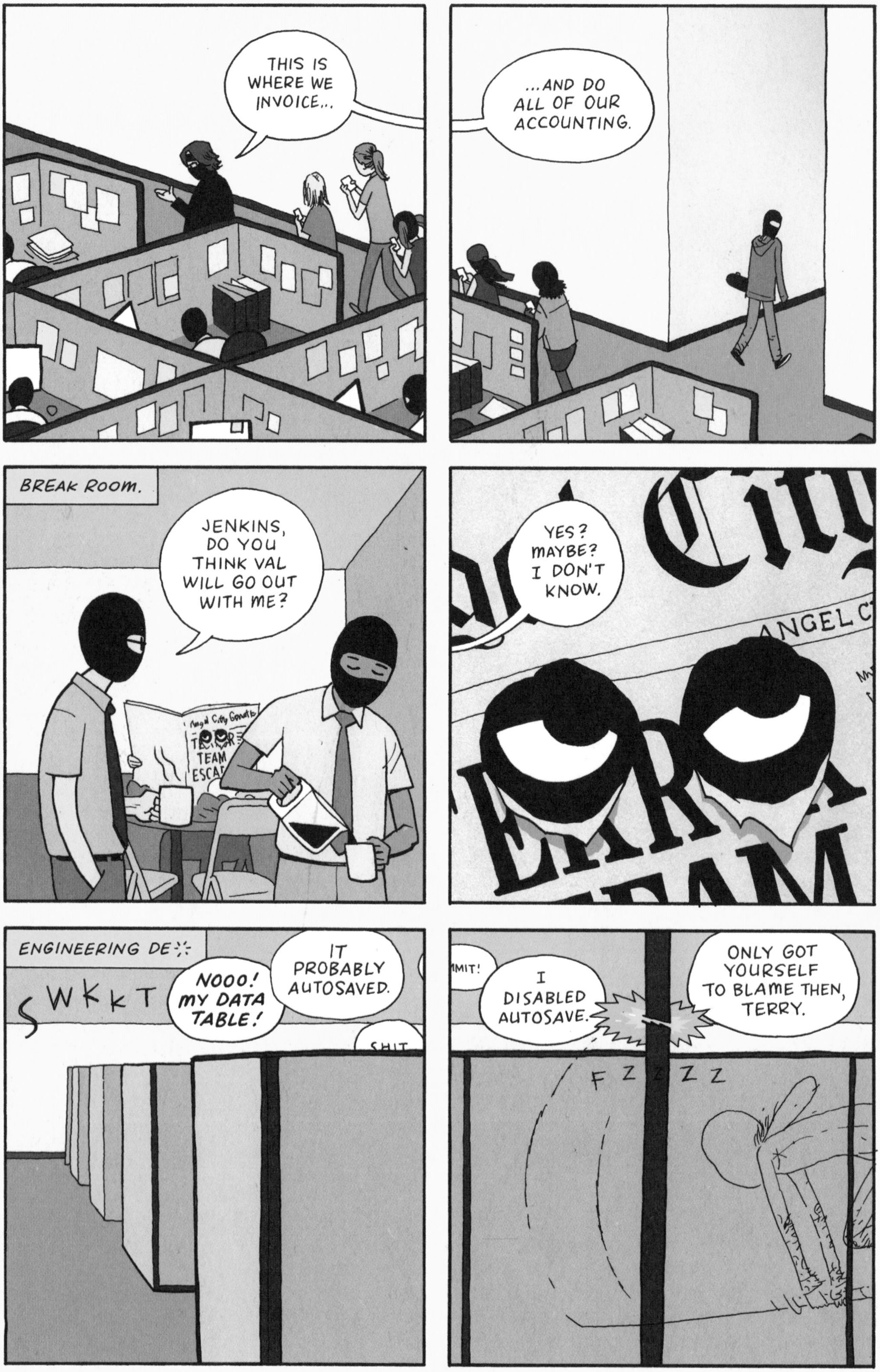
THIS IS WHERE WE INVOICE...
...AND DO ALL OF OUR ACCOUNTING.
BREAK ROOM.
JENKINS, DO YOU THINK VAL WILL GO OUT WITH ME?
YES? MAYBE? I DON'T KNOW.
ENGINEERING DE
SWKKT
NOOO! MY DATA TABLE!
IT PROBABLY AUTOSAVED.
MMIT!
I DISABLED AUTOSAVE.
ONLY GOT YOURSELF TO BLAME THEN, TERRY.
FZZZZ

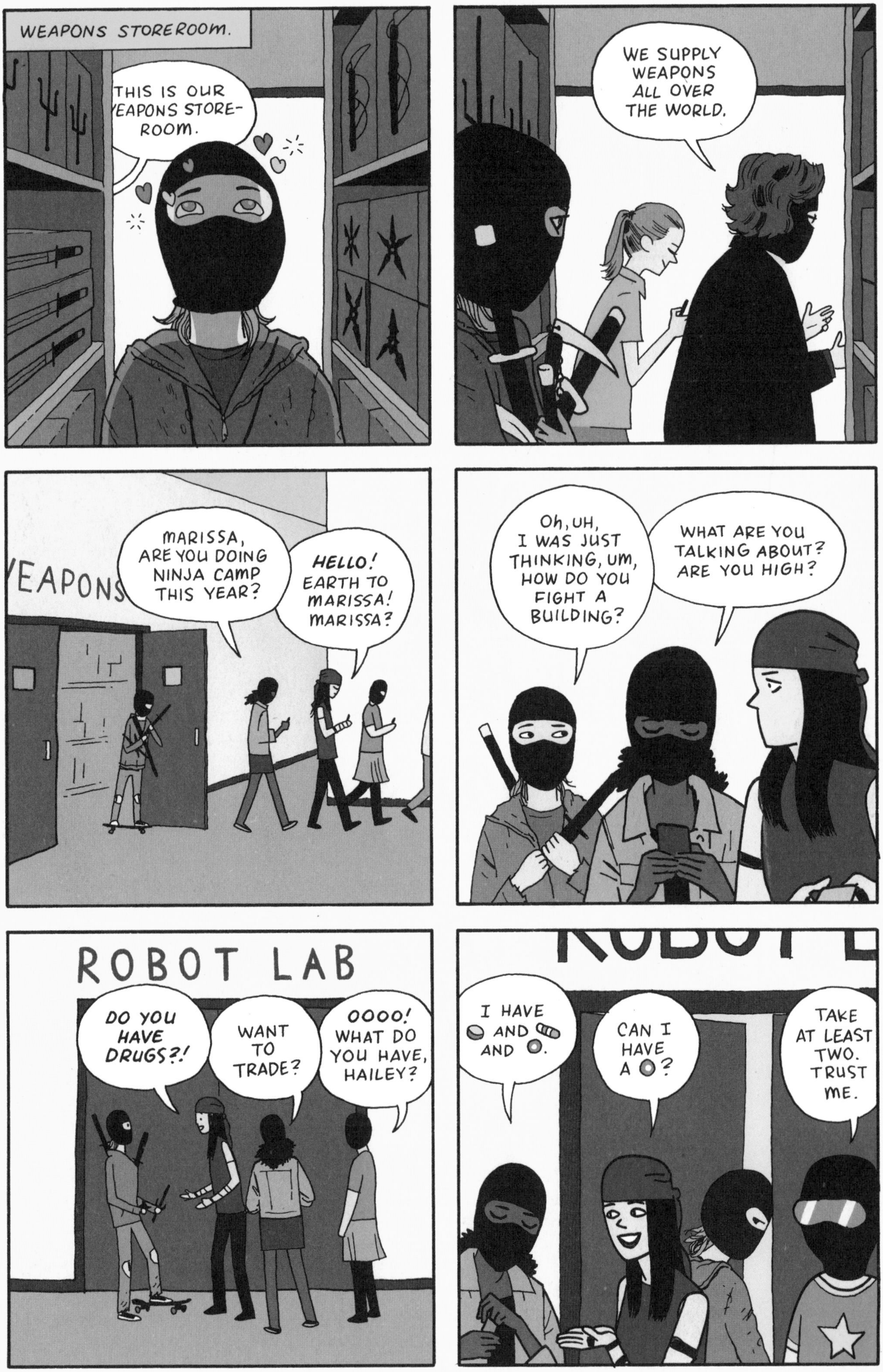
WEAPONS STOREROOM.
THIS IS OUR WEAPONS STORE-ROOM.
WE SUPPLY WEAPONS ALL OVER THE WORLD.
MARISSA, ARE YOU DOING NINJA CAMP THIS YEAR?
HELLO! EARTH TO MARISSA! MARISSA?
Oh, UH, I WAS JUST THINKING, UM, HOW DO YOU FIGHT A BUILDING?
WHAT ARE YOU TALKING ABOUT? ARE YOU HIGH?
ROBOT LAB
DO YOU HAVE DRUGS?!
WANT TO TRADE?
OOOO! WHAT DO YOU HAVE, HAILEY?
I HAVE AND AND .
CAN I HAVE A ?
TAKE AT LEAST TWO. TRUST ME.

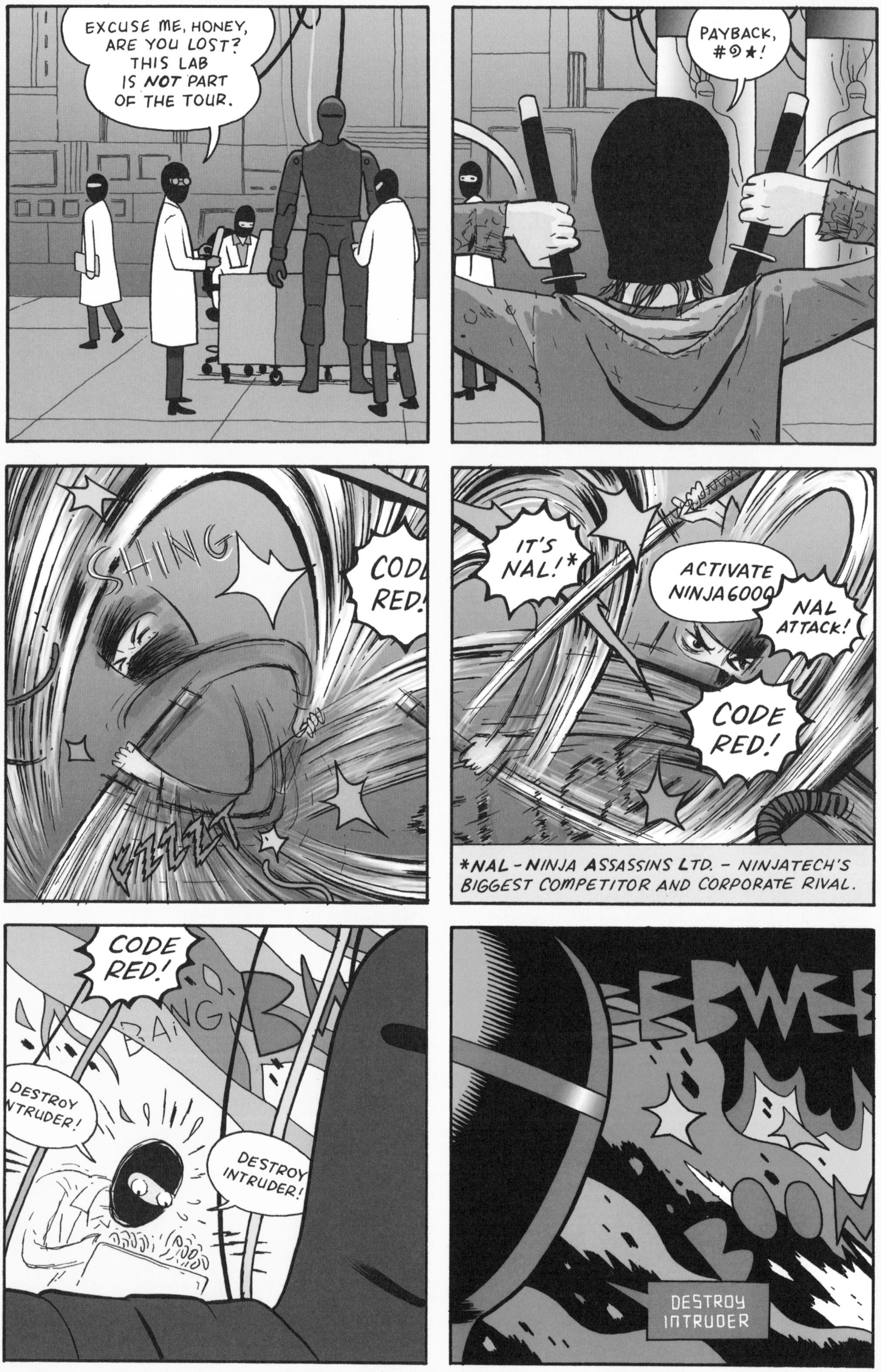
EXCUSE ME, HONEY, ARE YOU LOST? THIS LAB IS NOT PART OF THE TOUR.
PAYBACK, #9★!
SHING
CODE RED!
IT'S NAL!*
ACTIVATE NINJA6000
NAL ATTACK!
CODE RED!
*NAL - NINJA ASSASSINS LTD. - NINJATECH'S BIGGEST COMPETITOR AND CORPORATE RIVAL.
CODE RED!
DESTROY INTRUDER!
DESTROY INTRUDER!
DESTROY INTRUDER

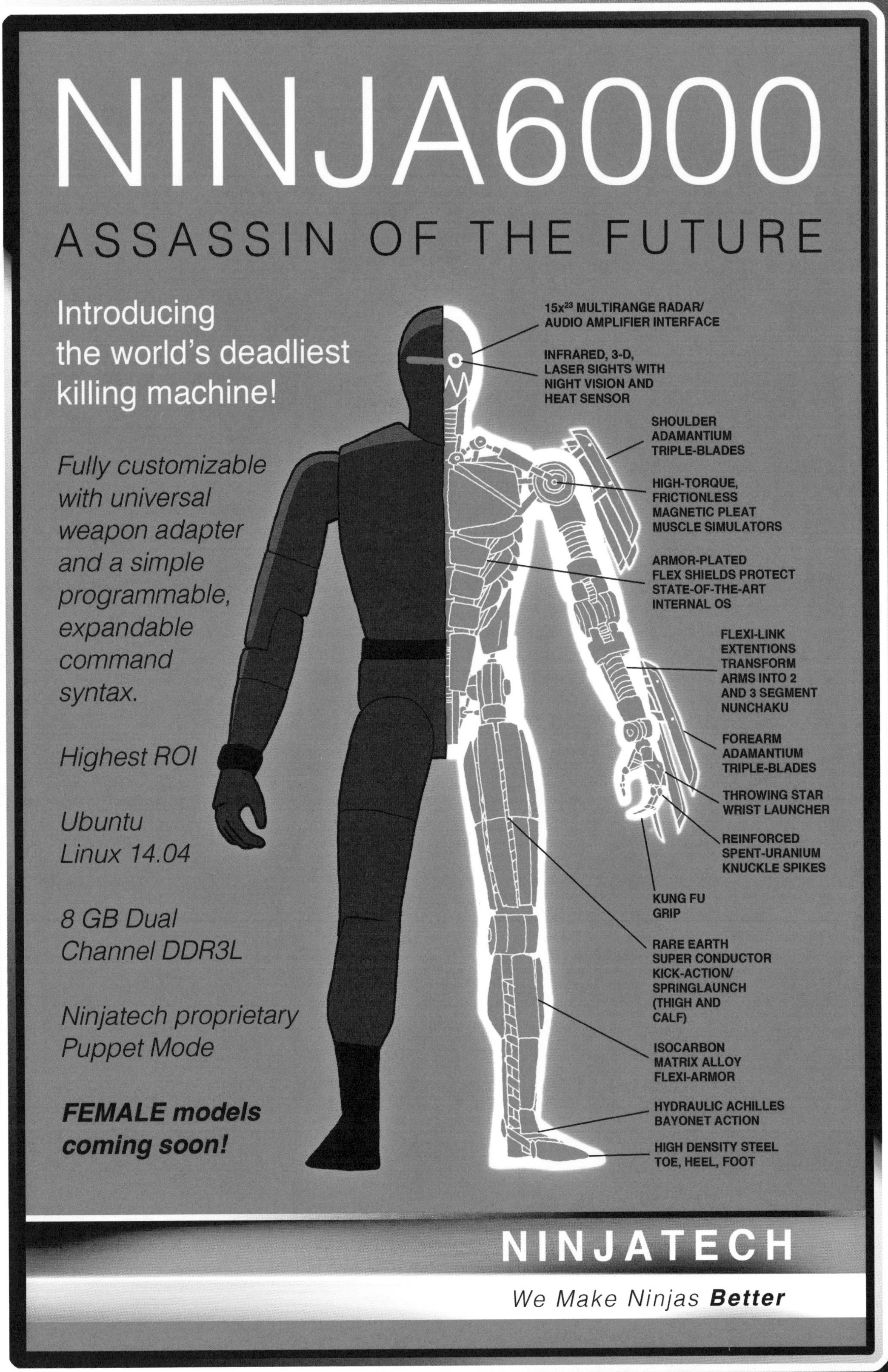

NINJA6000
ASSASSIN OF THE FUTURE
Introducing the world's deadliest killing machine!
Fully customizable with universal weapon adapter and a simple programmable, expandable command syntax.
Highest ROI
Ubuntu Linux 14.04
8 GB Dual Channel DDR3L
Ninjatech proprietary Puppet Mode
FEMALE models coming soon!
$15x^{23}$ MULTIRANGE RADAR/ AUDIO AMPLIFIER INTERFACE
INFRARED, 3-D, LASER SIGHTS WITH NIGHT VISION AND HEAT SENSOR
SHOULDER ADAMANTIUM TRIPLE-BLADES
HIGH-TORQUE, FRICTIONLESS MAGNETIC PLEAT MUSCLE SIMULATORS
ARMOR-PLATED FLEX SHIELDS PROTECT STATE-OF-THE-ART INTERNAL OS
FLEXI-LINK EXTENTIONS TRANSFORM ARMS INTO 2 AND 3 SEGMENT NUNCHAKU
FOREARM ADAMANTIUM TRIPLE-BLADES
THROWING STAR WRIST LAUNCHER
REINFORCED SPENT-URANIUM KNUCKLE SPIKES
KUNG FU GRIP
RARE EARTH SUPER CONDUCTOR KICK-ACTION/ SPRINGLAUNCH (THIGH AND CALF)
ISOCARBON MATRIX ALLOY FLEXI-ARMOR
HYDRAULIC ACHILLES BAYONET ACTION
HIGH DENSITY STEEL TOE, HEEL, FOOT
NINJATECH
We Make Ninjas Better

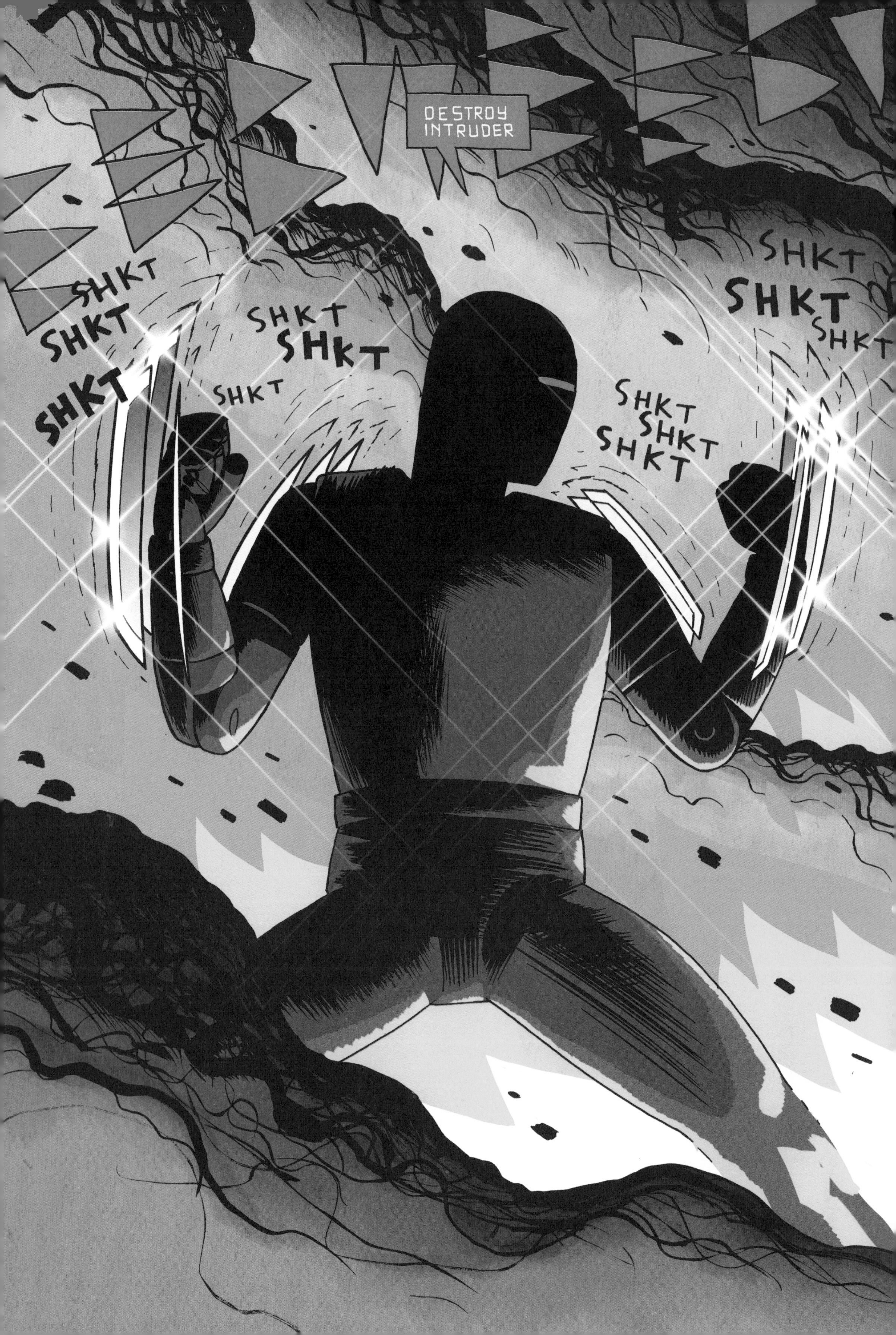
DESTROY INTRUDER
SHKT
SHKT
SHKT
SHKT
SHKT
SHKT
SHKT
SHKT
SHKT
SHKT
SHKT
SHKT
SHKT

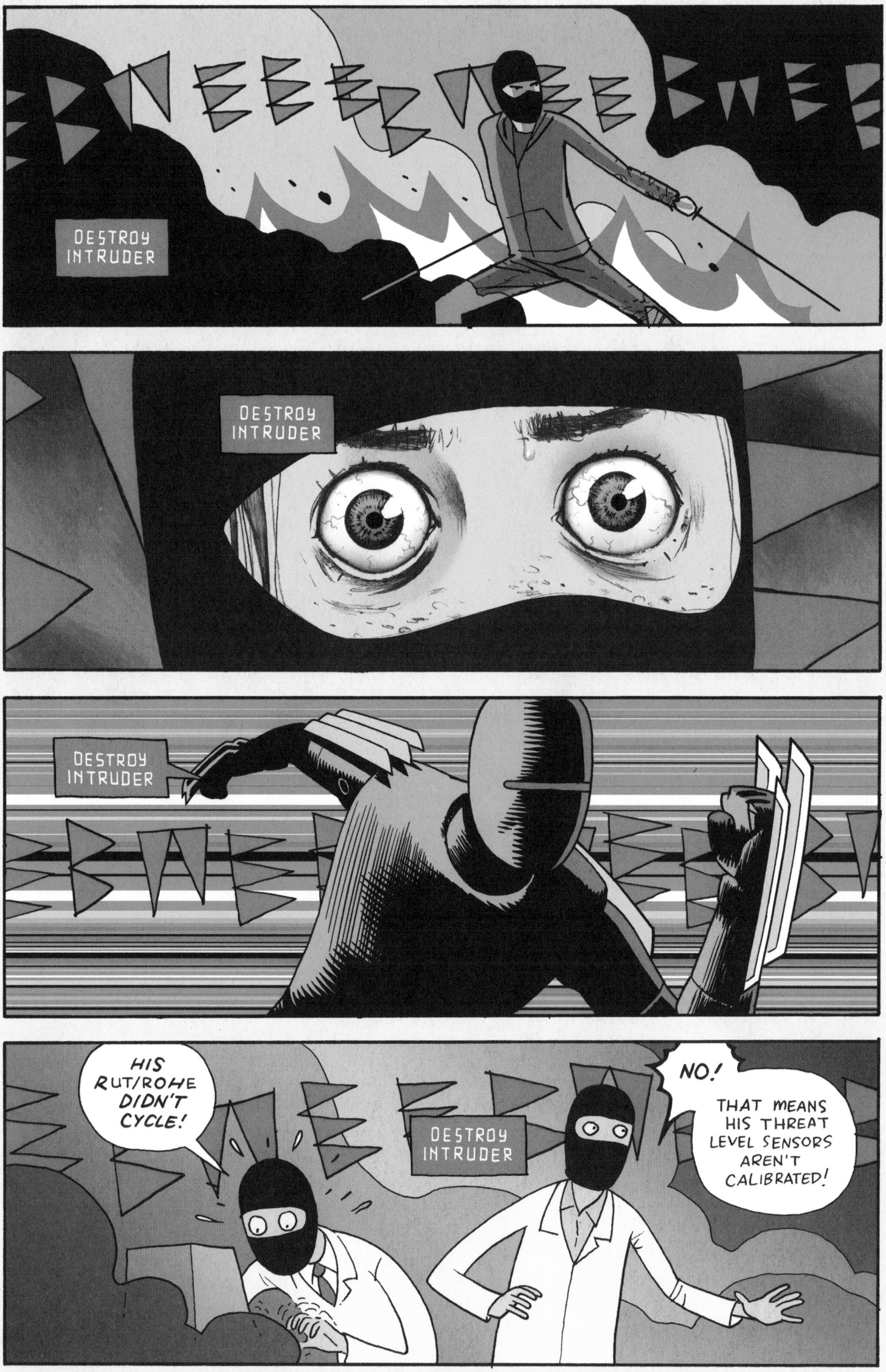
DESTROY INTRUDER
DESTROY INTRUDER
DESTROY INTRUDER
HIS RUT/ROHE DIDN'T CYCLE!
DESTROY INTRUDER
NO!
THAT MEANS HIS THREAT LEVEL SENSORS AREN'T CALIBRATED!

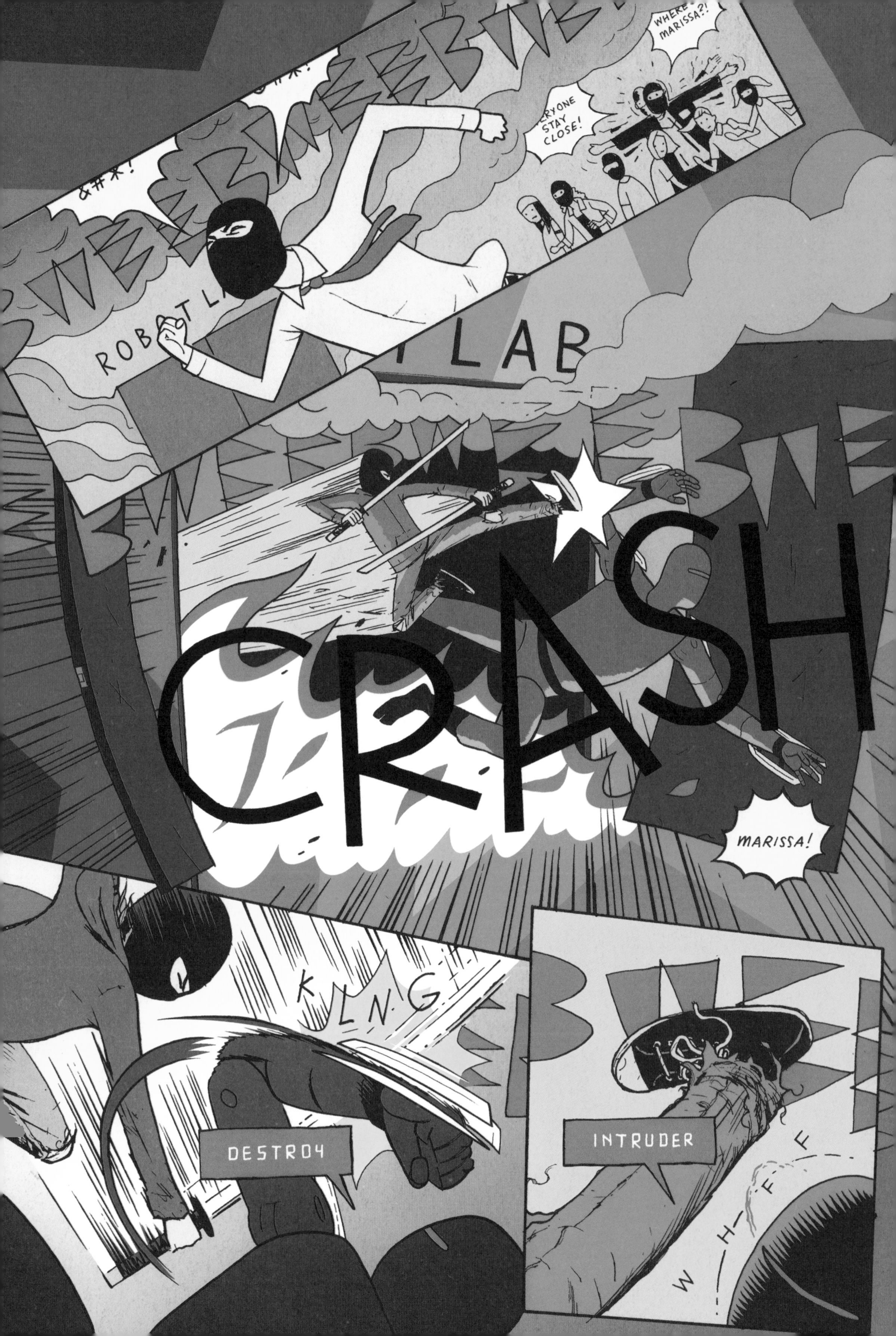
&#*!
ROBOTL
LAB
ERYONE STAY CLOSE!
WHERE MARISSA?!
CRASH
MARISSA!
KLNG
DESTROY
INTRUDER
WHFF

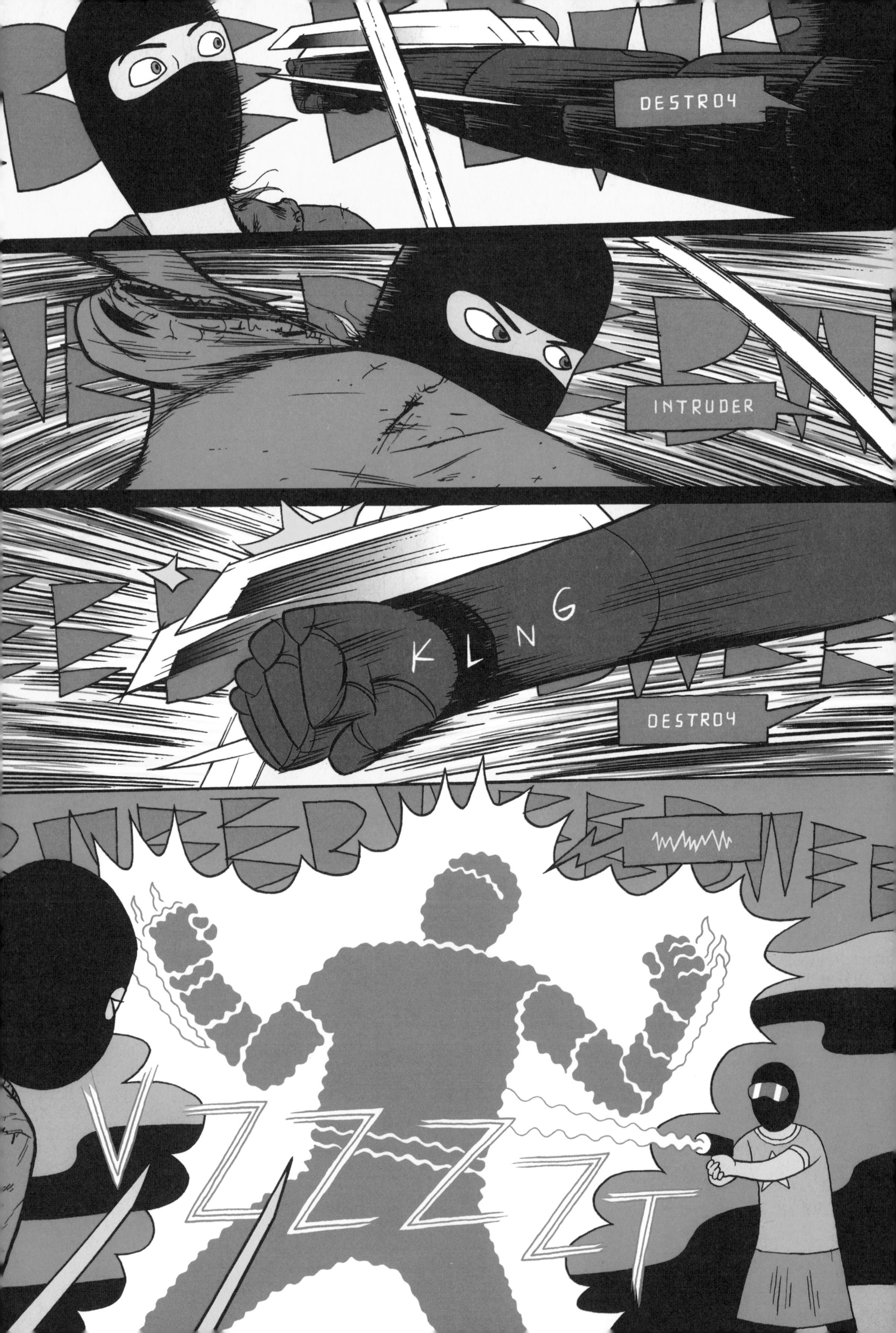
DESTROY
INTRUDER
KLNG
DESTROY
VZZZZT

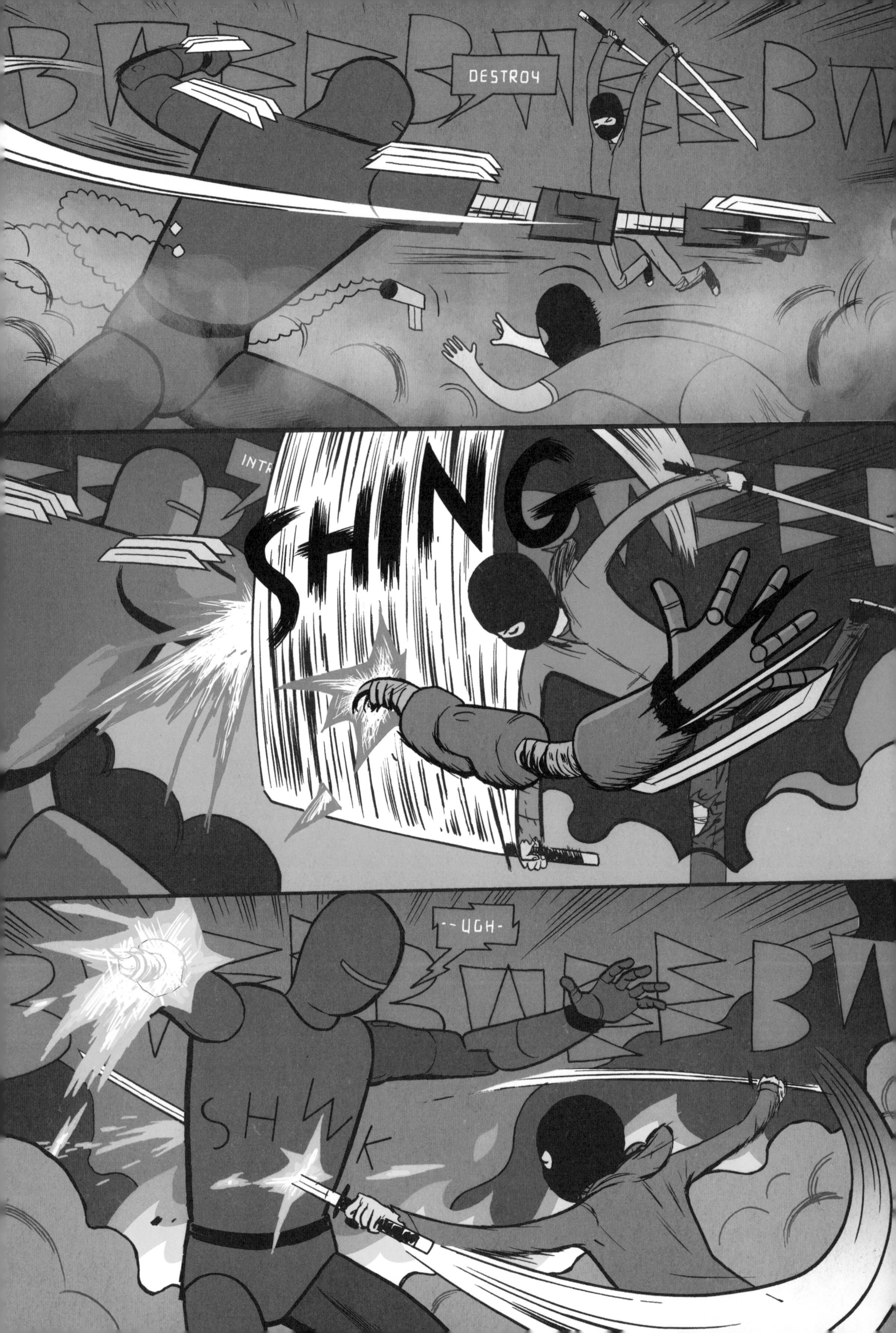
DESTROY
INTR
SHING
--UGH-
SHWK

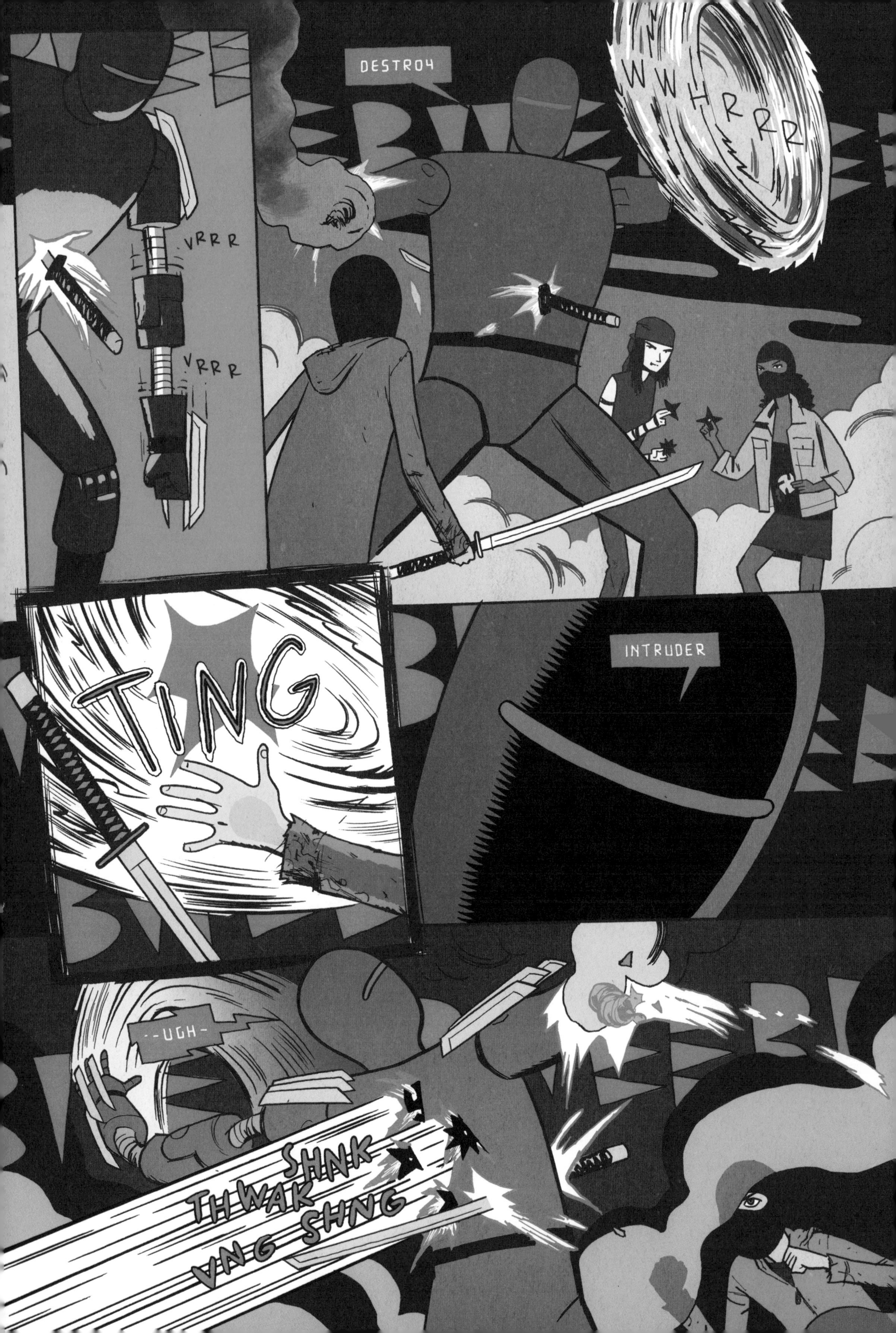
VRRR
VRRR
DESTROY
WWHRRRR
TING
INTRUDER
-UGH-
SHNK
THWAK
VNG SHNG

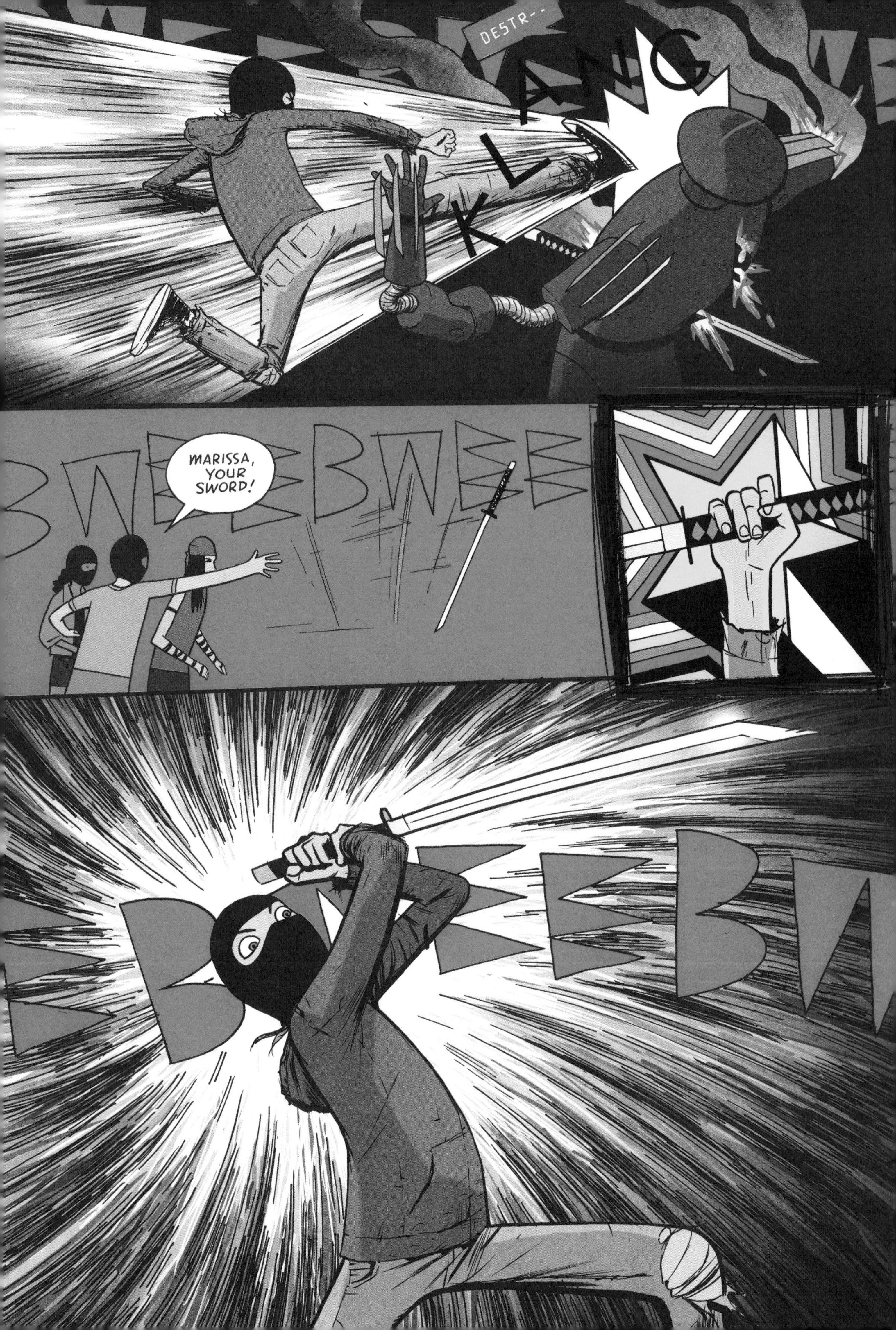
DESTR--
KLANG
MARISSA, YOUR SWORD!

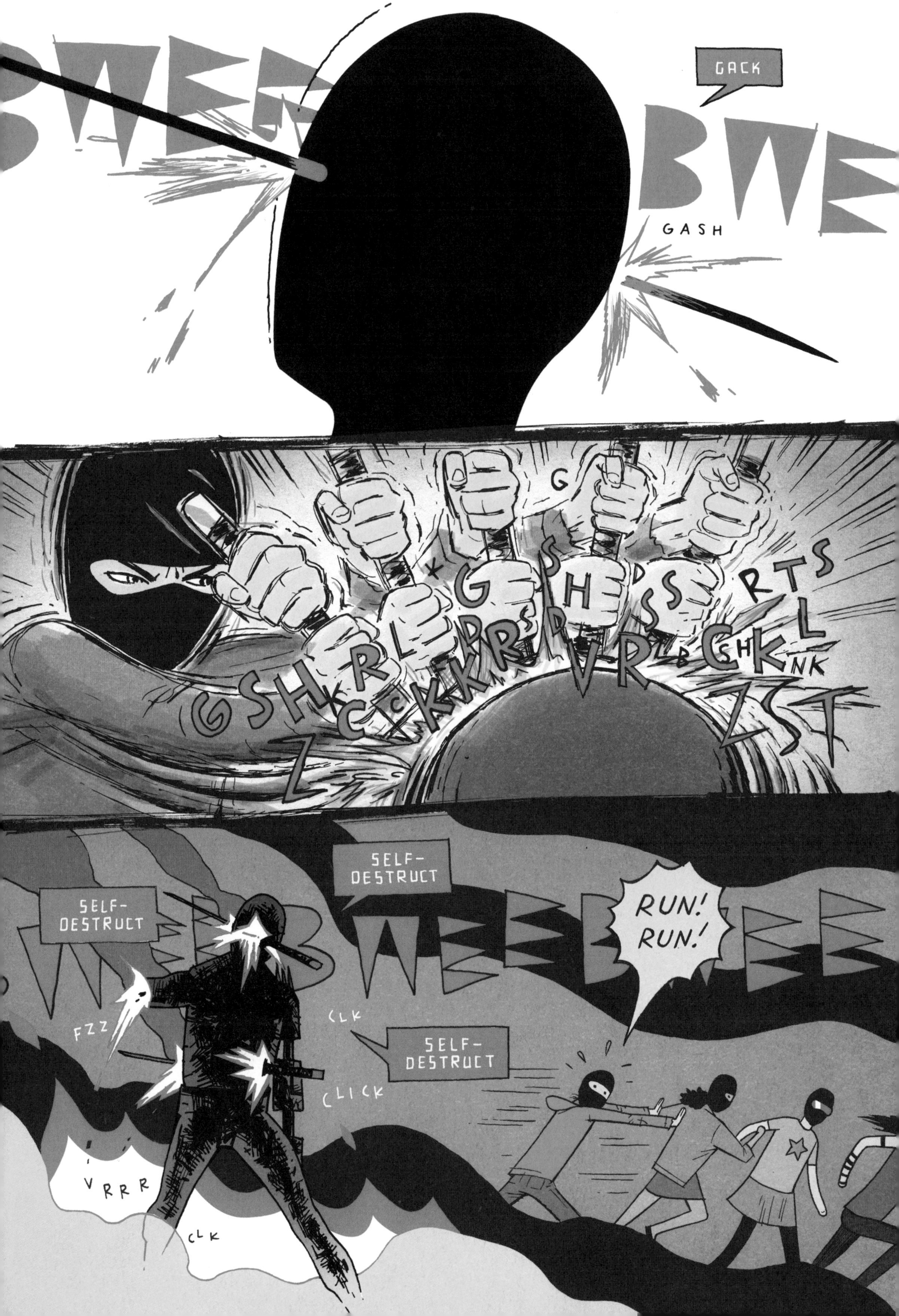
GACK
BWE
GASH
SELF-
DESTRUCT
SELF-
DESTRUCT
RUN!
RUN!
FZZ
CLK
SELF-
DESTRUCT
CLICK
VRRR
CLK

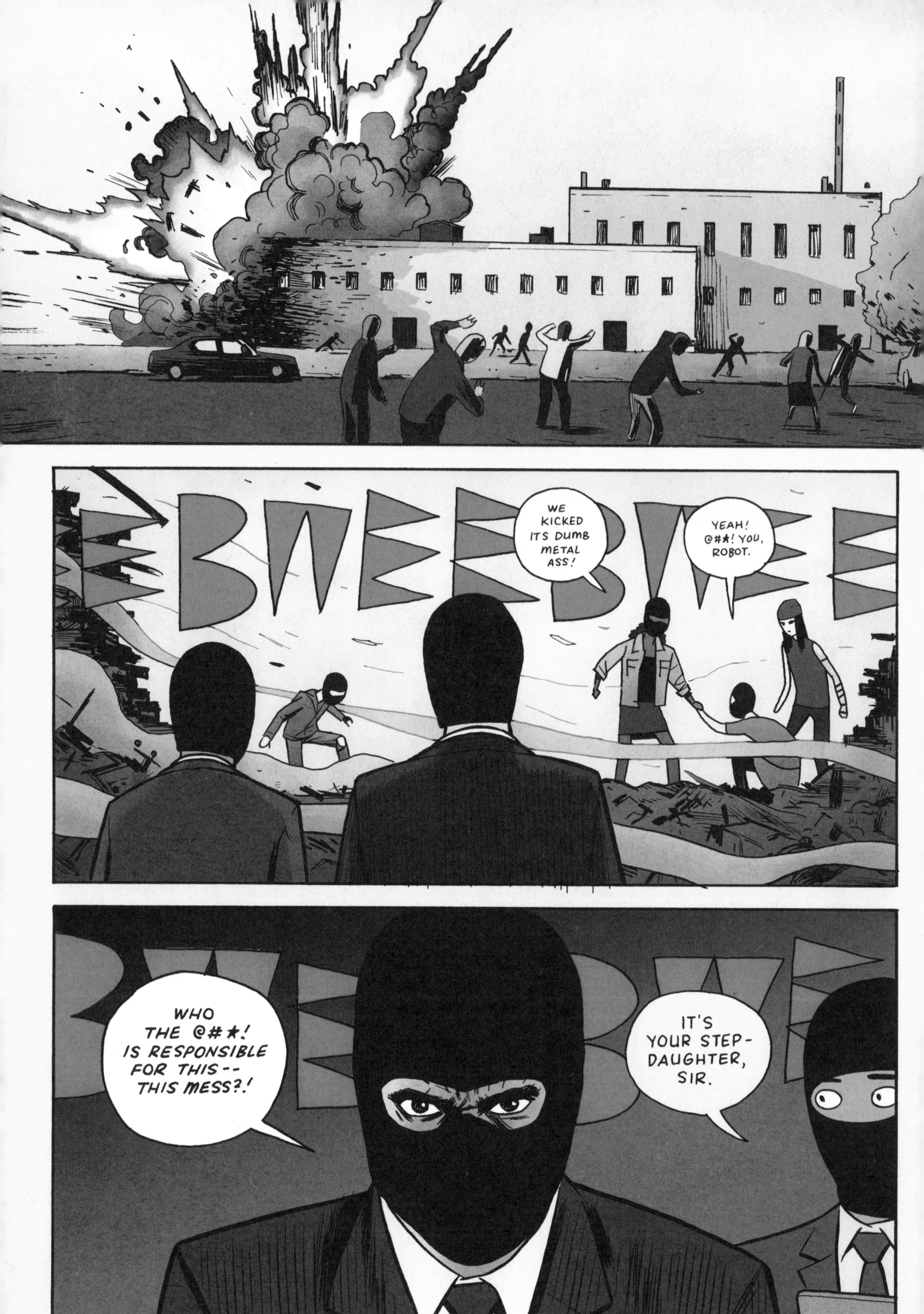
WE KICKED ITS DUMB METAL ASS!
YEAH! @#★! YOU, ROBOT.
WHO THE @#★! IS RESPONSIBLE FOR THIS-- THIS MESS?!
IT'S YOUR STEP-DAUGHTER, SIR.

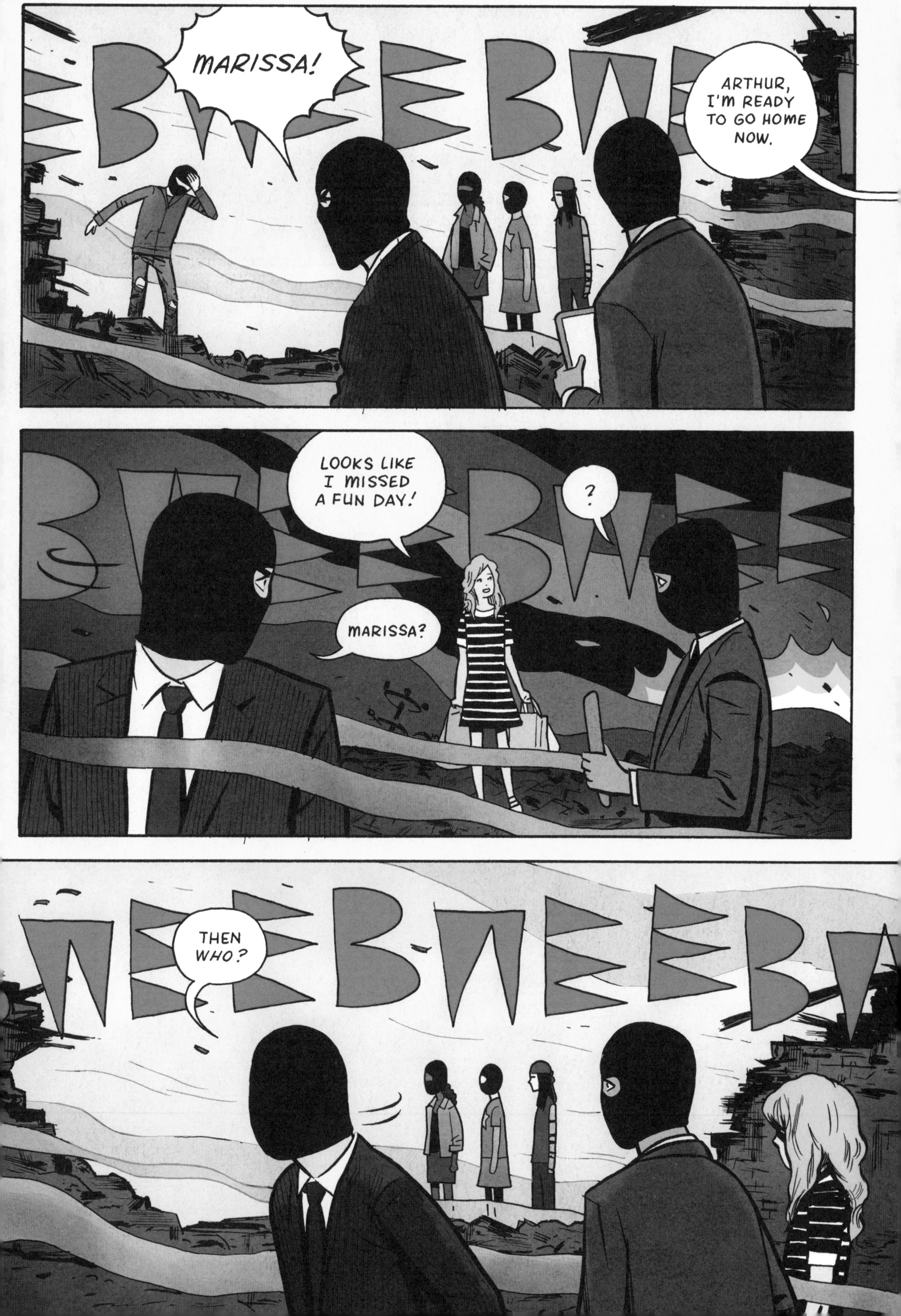
MARISSA!
ARTHUR, I'M READY TO GO HOME NOW.
LOOKS LIKE I MISSED A FUN DAY!
?
MARISSA?
THEN WHO?

The End

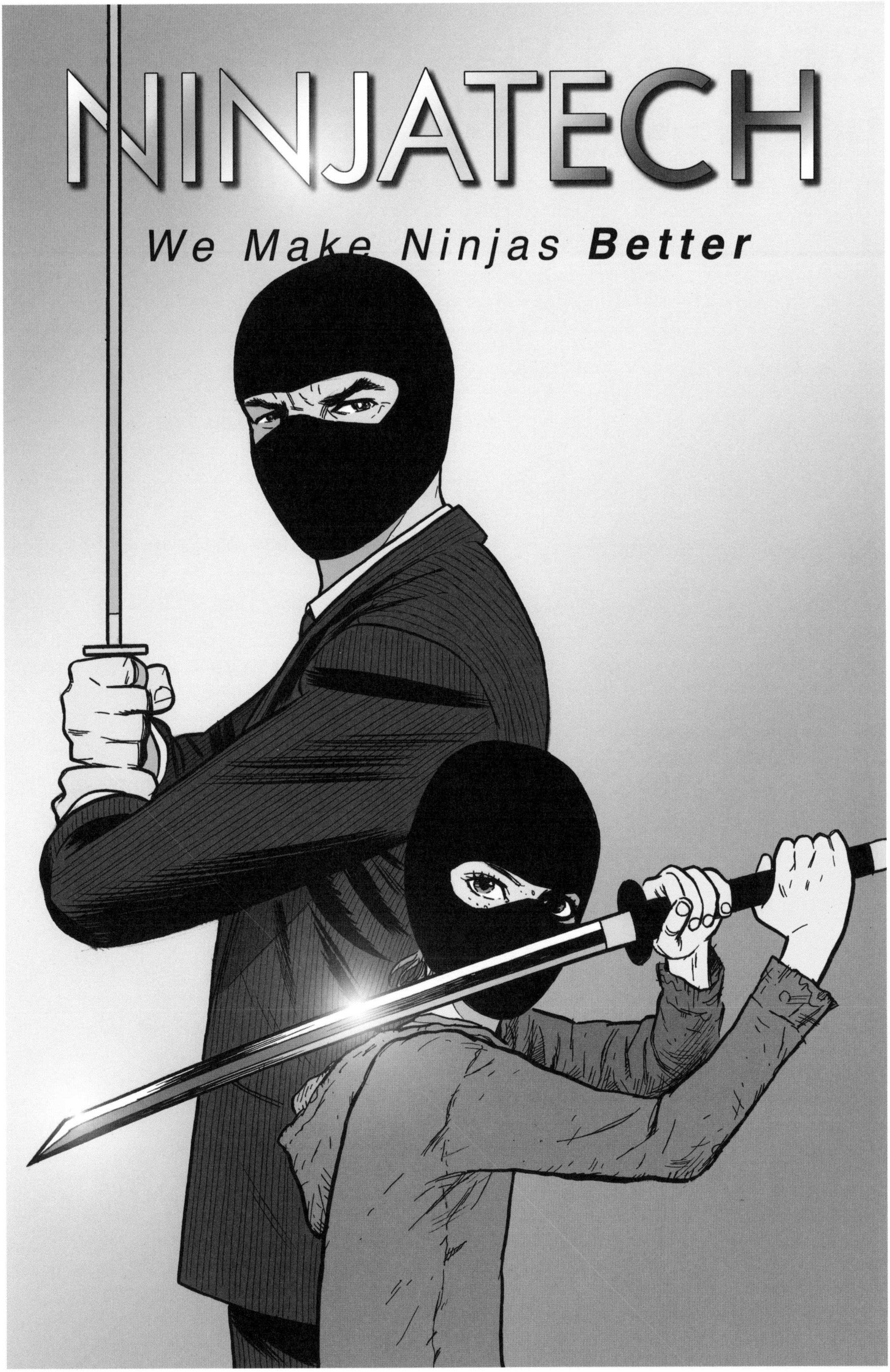
NINJATECH
We Make Ninjas Better

Book Club | Classroom Discussion Questions

01. What is your favorite kind of donut?

02. What do you want to be when you grow up?

03. Do you know what your parents do at their jobs?

04. Butterfly knife or nunchuck?

05. Do you think the military industrial complex already has advanced ninja-robots like the Ninja-6000?

06. Should 2nd Amendment right to bear arms include ninja weapons?

07. True / False - Ben Franklin was the first American Ninja.

08. Best Master: Splinter, Stick, John Peter McAllistar, Mr Miyagi, Ninjor

09. Would you rather fight a ninja or a polar bear? Why?

10. Best Movie: Ninja III: The Domination, Beverly Hills Ninja, Enter the Ninja, Teenage Mutant Ninja Turtles 2: The Secret of the Ooze, Ninja Scroll

11. The ninja-werewolf you created escapes from your lab and all it wants is to kill the person that gave it the peculiar agony of life. What do you do?

12. How many points does your favorite throwing star have?

13. If you could hire a ninja, what would you have her do?

14. Do ninjas exist?

15. Have you ever given someone a karate chop? Why?

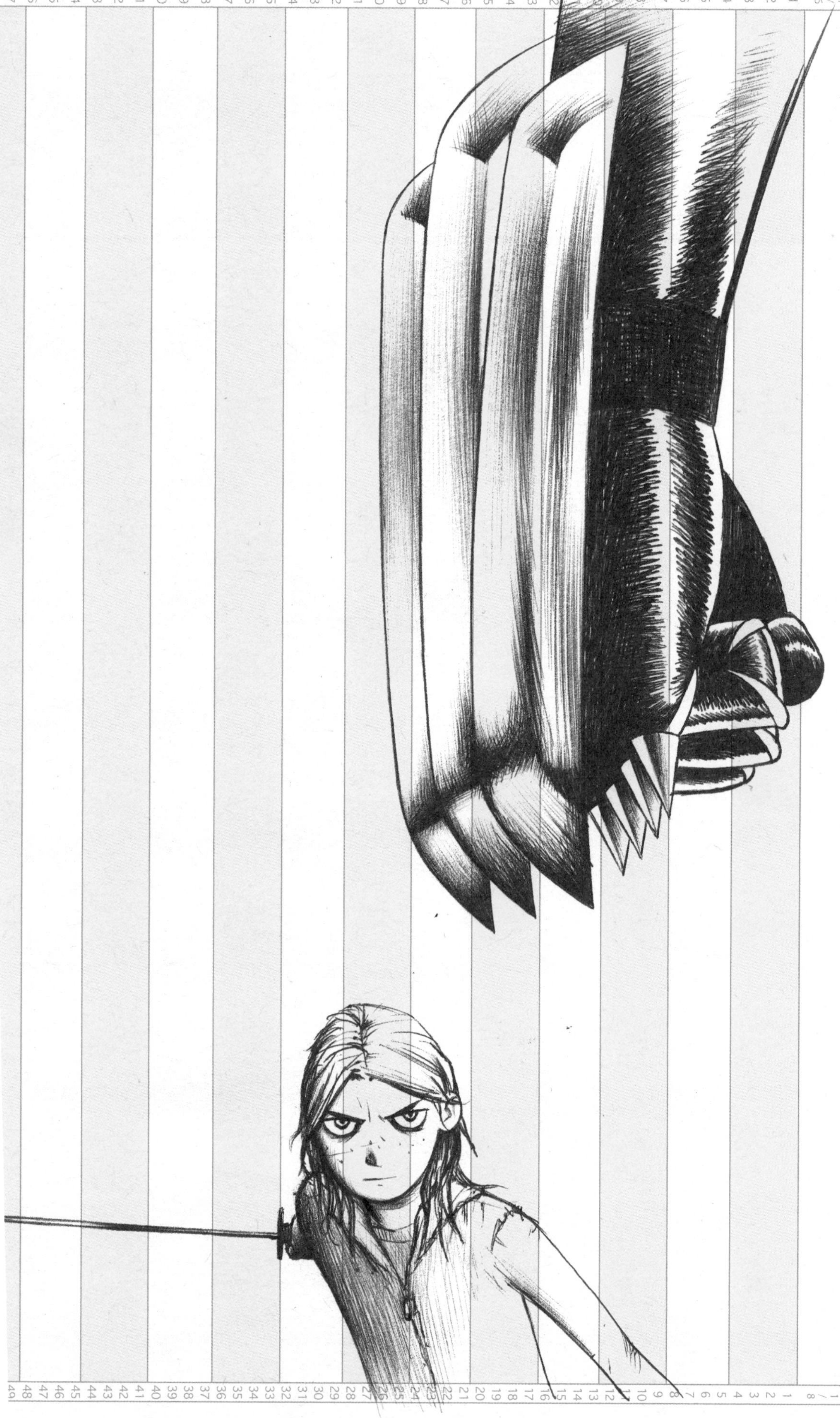

Carl runs away...

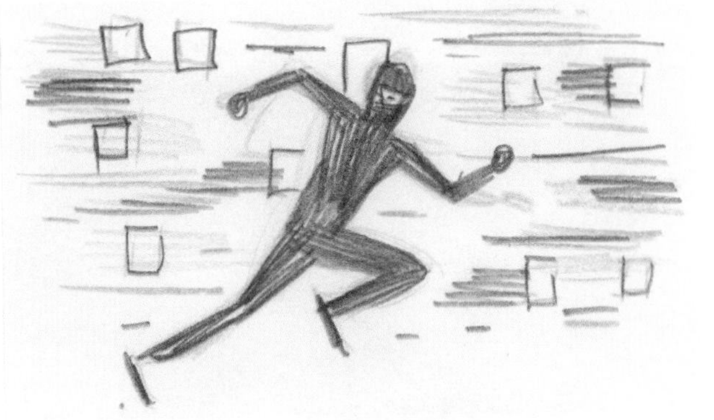

"Ninja Carl runs for all he's worth. He steals a motorcycle, hides on a cargo ship, runs past the Eiffel Tower and pyramids, eventually, he ends up at some monastery in the Himalayan mountains."

Usually Jim and Brian write a detailed panel-by-panel script. But for this sequence they only wrote the paragraph above. Then Jim sketched Carl in various states of flight on index cards so he could easily compose and edit the scene by moving the cards around.

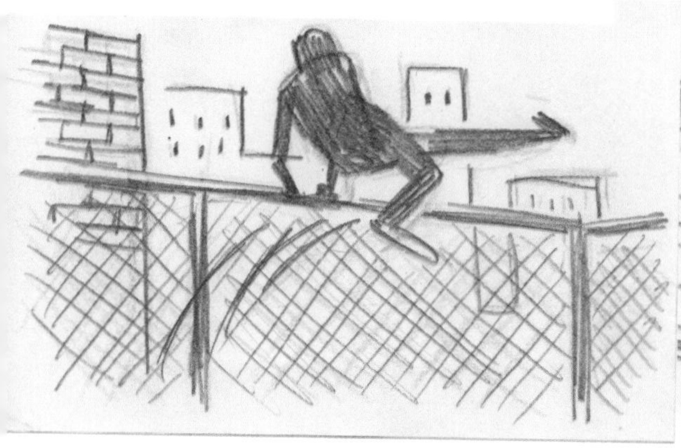

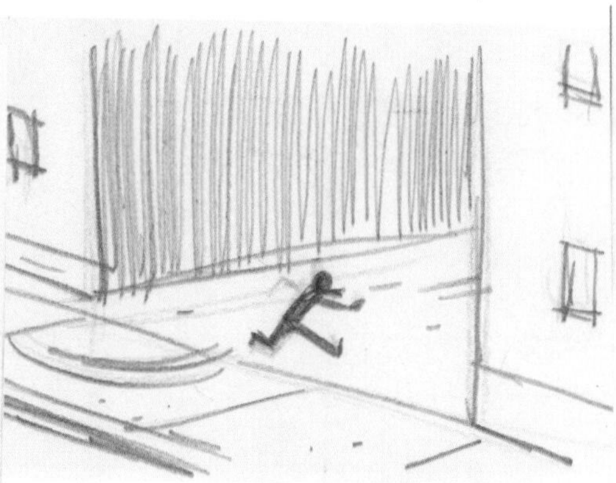

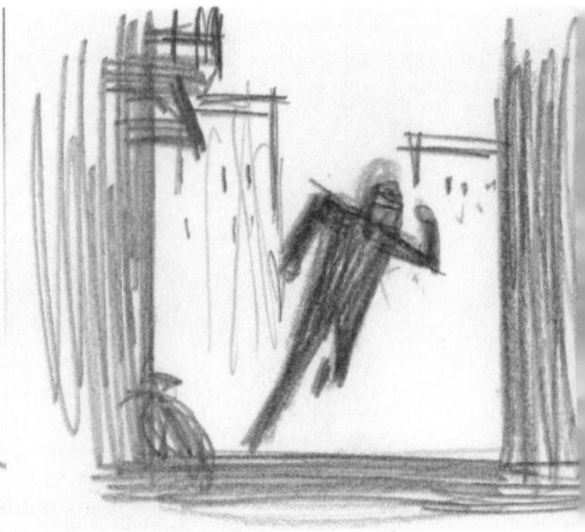

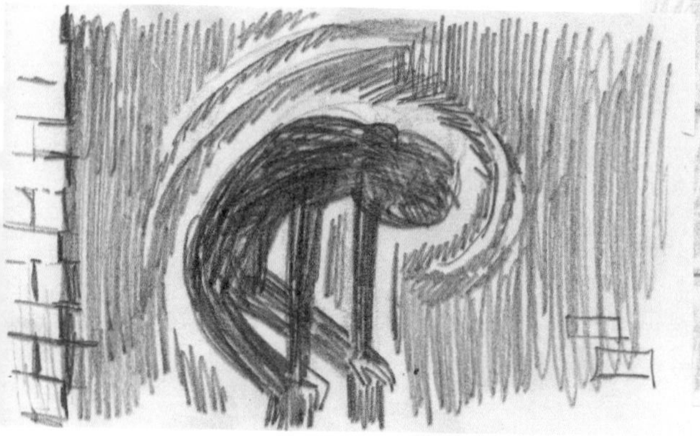

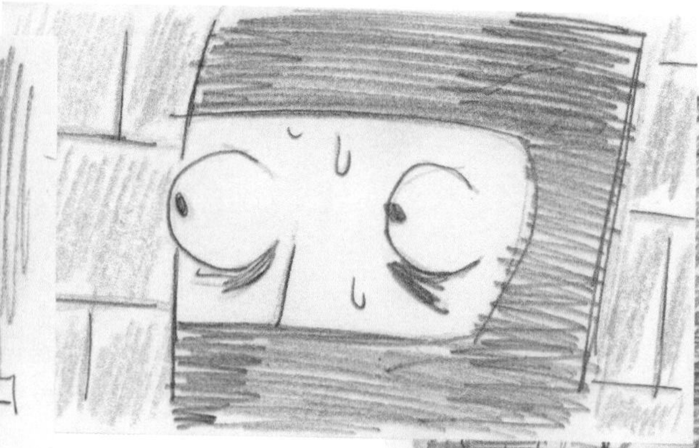

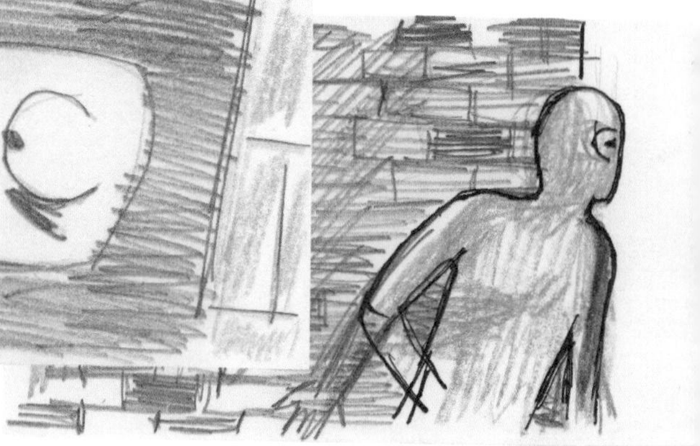

Alternative ideas for this sequence:

1. Fashion the page like a board game, for example - Life or Chutes and Ladders. In this style, there could be little bits of text that detail Carl running for his life.

2. This could be Carl's entire life story. He runs away. Eventually he finds peace. He becomes a different person entirely. Maybe it's something noble - he helps Ninjas rehab and become contributing members of society. Maybe it's nothing - he takes on a false identity and ends up working at Walmart, falls in love, has a couple kids, suburban boredom, eventually grows old and dies.

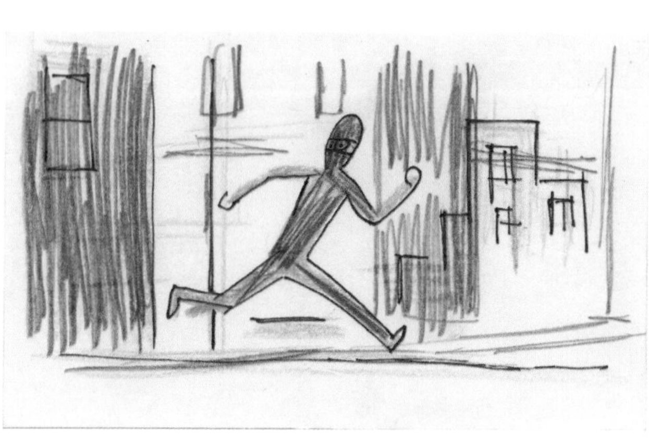

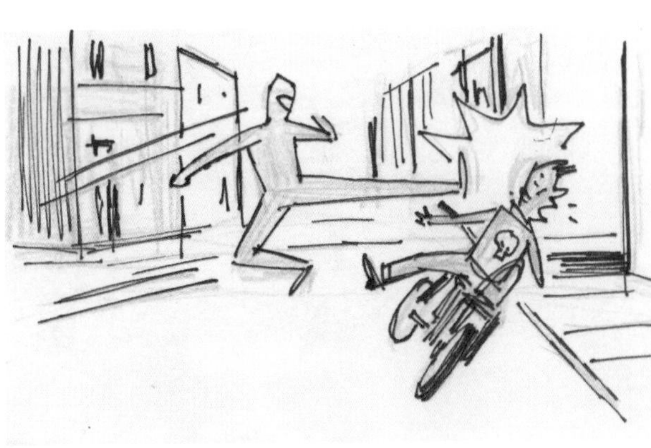

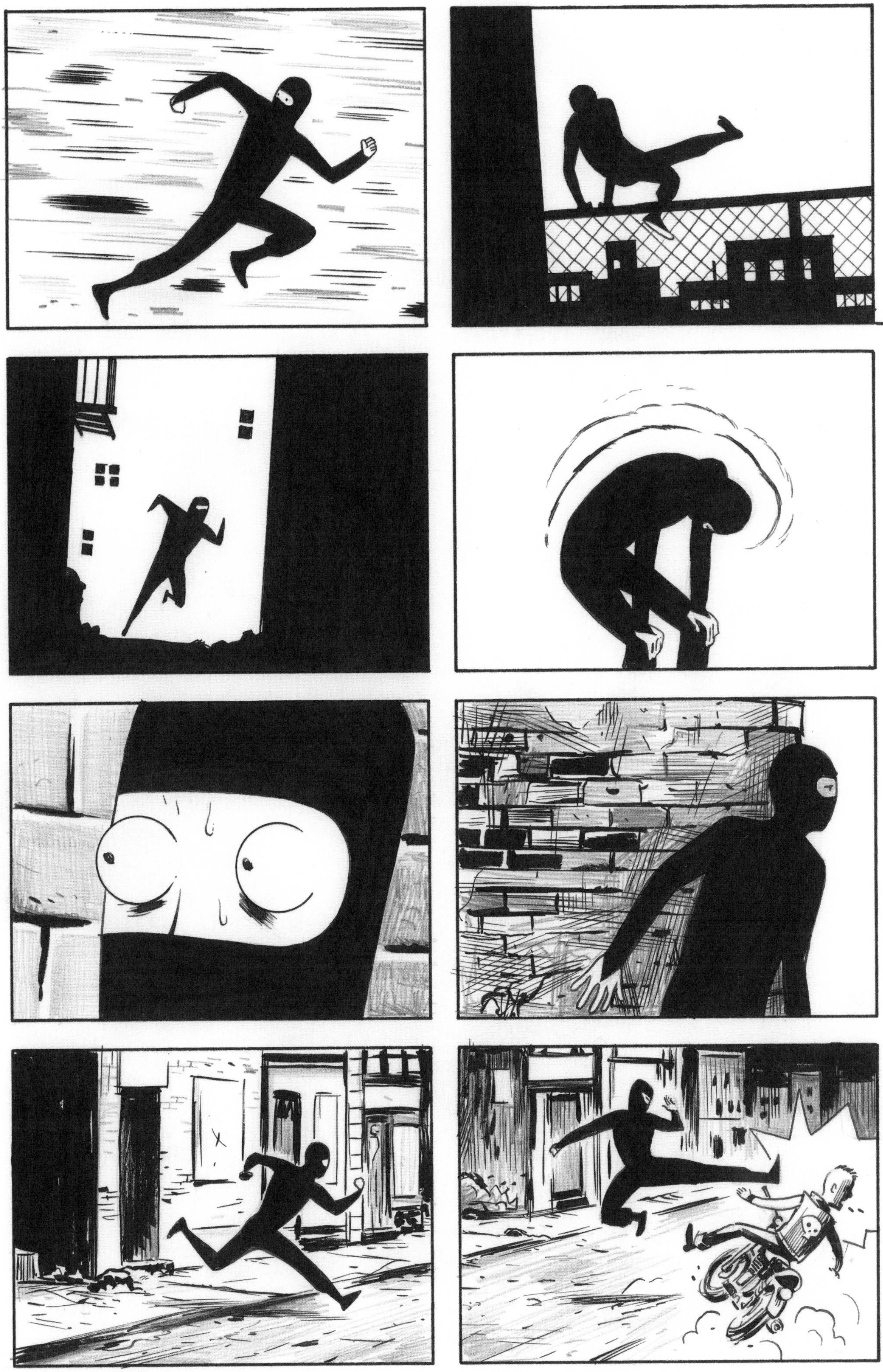

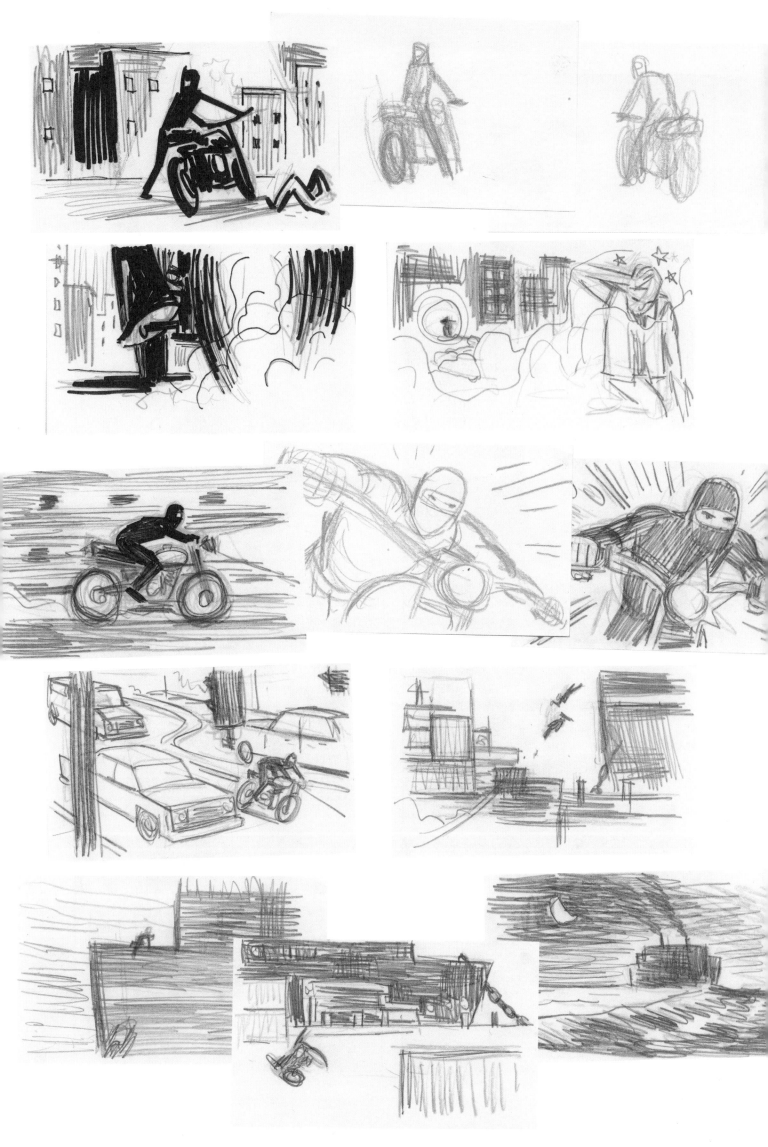

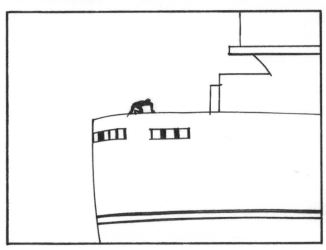

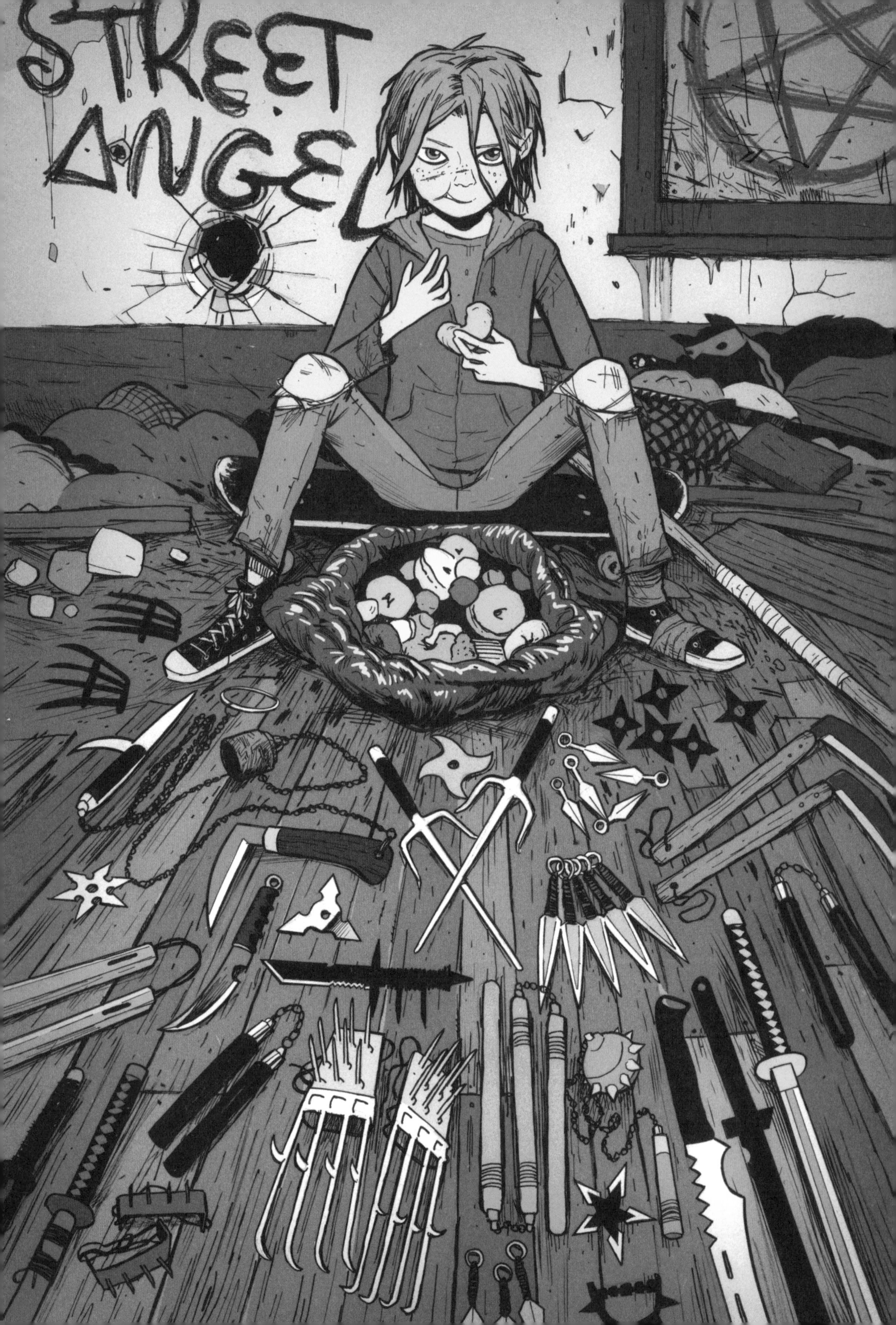
STREET
ANGEL

Street Angel Glossary

[Redacted] Labs: One of many clandestine labs dealing in super science in Wilksboro. Bankrolled by Diablo Enterprises.

*V: IPF agent assigned to earth. Friends with Bell, Lilith, and Emma. Jesse is not a fan.

Afrodite: See Aliyah Jefferson.

Alcatraz, Jr.: The world's highest security juvenile detention center. Located conveniently in Wilksboro.

Aliyah Jefferson: Van Buren Middle School's principal by day, Wilksboro's vigilante-protector (as Afrodite) at night.

Angel City Hospital: It's just a hospital...nothing nefarious goes on here...except that J-horror puppet master/ghost dustup. Otherwise just healing people up, yep.

Armstrong: Angel City's original protector. Believed to be dead (he isn't - just short a few screws and legs and arm).

The Assassin's Tower: Posh apartment tower in central Wilksboro housing the world's most dangerous assassins.

Atomic Taco: Taco joint. Street Angel gets a discount.

Avalanchia: Dr. Pangea's granddaughter. Quite evil.

The Bakery Boys: Bear Claw and Jimmies. One is dumb and the other is jimmies. Young, naive, they believe there was a golden age of supervillainy.

Bald Eagle: Crazy homeless one-limbed skateboard beggar. Maybe an ex-superhero? Jesse's right-hand man (it's the only hand he has).

Big Ed: Proprietor of the obviously named Big Ed's. Edna is a lady who has built her reputation on never taking any $#!+. She also makes a pretty tasty selection of snacks.

Big Ed's: Hangout Speakeasy run by Big Ed (naturally). One of the few sanctuary spots in Wilksboro. The Bald Eagle enjoys hanging out here (rumor has it that he and Big Ed were an item).

Bell: Charlie Bellweather, Jesse's best friend and super military advanced robot on the lam. She is unaware of the robot, military, and the lam parts. [previously Maxine Bell, previously Bell Blake, certainly not a naming mistake on our part - stupid editor...]

Black Alice: Street witch. Take care that you don't mix up your "w"s and "b"s.

Bleeders: Legendary Wilksboro street gang. Word on the street is that they messed with the wrong person and are no longer active.

Bloody Mary's: The number 1 Mary-themed gang in Wilksboro.

Brian Maruca: Co-creator of STREET ANGEL. Never-finder of Easter eggs. Loves hyperbole more than absolutely anything else in the world.

Captain Alpha: Angel City's superhero protector. He's practically perfect in every way. Jesse hates him.

Complicated-Trap-Man: Real name, Herbert Goldberg. Number of traps effectively sprung? 0...but c'mon, they're complicated.

Cyberlords: The second most dangerous street gang in Wilksboro. Technologically enhanced.

Desmond Carter: Millionaire playboy and controlling interest in Diablo Enterprises. See also: The Devil (1).

The Devil (1): Angel City's feared and revered vigilante. Is he fighting crime or inciting it? See also: Desmond Carter. Also, not to be confused with the actual Devil.

The Devil (2): Literally, like, the devil, aka Lucifer, aka Satan. Just the worst. Lilith's dad.

Discount Labs: "Science" at a discount. Might cost you an arm but you'll keep your legs.

Dr. Bell: Bell's father. He discovered X-731 alone in a lab and freed the girl and escaped to Wilksboro. He dabbles in super science while keeping a low profile as a janitor.

Dr. Pangea: The world's most dangerous geologist. Currently incarcerated.

Dynamites: An all elementary school kid gang. Kind of like the minor leagues for gangs.

Emma: The third member of Jesse's school buddies. Zombie, both classically and socially. Infected with zombinol.

Father Josh Manly: The only good priest in WB. Teaches shop at Van Buren. Jesus in disguise but he's just here to teach again and hopefully not let things get out of control like last time.

Food For Thought: Wilksboro charitable food bank. The fewer questions the better.

Forbidden Zone: One square block in the middle of Wilksboro's central park. It's the result of a science experiment gone wrong. Although one square block from the outside, it's huge on the inside. Various monsters and/or monsterized animals lurk in the zone's super fertile forest.

The Fort: A giant complex of buildings that have slowly merged into a small city. It started out as government housing in the 60s and has become a self-sustaining city run by a gangster.

IPF: The Intergalactic Peace Force. Alien police force that patrols the galaxy to ensure that peace reigns. So far so good (intergalactically speaking)!

Jacob Cassidy: The Ninja Kid! A fellow 7th grader at Van Buren. The only known person to defeat Jesse in a fair* fight. *Rumor has it that it was fixed.

Jesse Sanchez: 7th grade student at ...who are we kidding! It's Street Angel! This is her book.

Jim Rugg: Cartoonist - STREET ANGEL, *Afrodisiac, PLAIN Janes.* Friend of cats. IG: *@jimruggart, jimrugg.com*

Jimmy Blade's Dungeon Arcade: An arcade. In Wilksboro. They can have some nice things, too. One of Jesse's hangouts.

Josey: One of many dogs that Jesse has befriended and terrified (cough, no prize, cough). Definitely not an early incarnation of Princess.

Juan: A 7th grader at Van Buren. He has a crush on Jesse (it is unrequited).

Lilith: One of Jesse's other school friends. Satan's daughter. She needed a break from her stepmother, Tiffany, and enrolled in Van Buren.

Lola The Young Vandal: 10 y.o. skateboarding street artist and member of the Bushwick Collective. OMG do I feel old.

Lou Nar: See The Moon.

M.A.R.Y.: Mechanized Armed Response Youth. Another robot that has escaped and found a home in Wilksboro. A member of the Bloody Marys (obviously).

Maria Madison: aka "Mad Dog". A decent kid with a troubled past.

Meatball (1): Ground beef mixed with bread, cheese (mozz and parm), garlic, eggs, and salt, formed into ball shapes and fried until crispy brown on the outside. Alt: same mix but cooked in the spaghetti sauce.

Meatball (2): Ninja Cat's dog nemesis. He is a bulldog.

MoA: The Museum of Awesome. National museum of superheroes and supervillains. Created by The Thinker, the man who could think objects into existence with his mind!

Miss Shannon: Van Buren school guidance counselor and makeshift psychologist.

The MOON: He's been circling the Earth for 50 million years, waiting to get his revenge.

Mother Superior: Top of the Wilksboro Nunja hierarchy. Scary. Aware of Jesse's dual identity. Ally inasmuch as Jesse keeps to the straight and narrow.

Ninja Cat: He is both a ninja and a cat. One of the good guys.

The Ninja Kid: See Jacob Cassidy.

Ninja 6000: The latest in technological innovation from NinjaTech.

NinjaTech: The leading supplier of ninja tech and ninja assets.

Nunchuck: She is both a ninja and a nun. One of the really bad guys. Separated from the Nunja to start her own nunja-style convent, the Blood Wimple.

Pizza: Round disc of dough topped with sauce, cheese, and your choice of toppings. It's a little more complicated than that but if you don't know what pizza is at this point in your life, there's not much I can do for you.

Priesthoods: Clergy-styled gang.

Princess: A little lost dog that Jesse befriends, terrifies*, and returns to her (human) family. *Not intentionally.

Rachel King: Troubled young lady currently serving time in Alcatraz, Jr. See Red Kite.

Red Kite: Rachel King's superhero alter ego. Previously Super Hawk's sidekick (and adopted daughter).

Serpentina: Snake lady. Nassssty.

Shiraz Thunderbird: Jesse's super secret alter alter ego.

Sister Soul: Arthur Jackson always wanted to be a nun when he grew up. When he lost his job, his boyfriend, and his family (they found out about his boyfriend), he moved to Wilksboro to live out his childhood dream. Unofficial Nunja.

Socrates Smith (human): Scientist. His consciousness was transferred into a dumpster in a science mishap.

Socrates Smith (dumpster): Ideal for medium-sized business or high-volume small businesses such as gas stations, convenience stores, or stores in a shopping mall.

6′ wide x 5.5′ deep x 4′ tall in the front slanting to 5′ tall in the back. Holds roughly 60 kitchen-sized (13 gallon) trash bags.

Street Angel: The deadliest girl alive! The Princess of Poverty! Fights evil...etc...etc...could she be mild-mannered student Jesse Sanchez? Yes. Weapon of choice: Skateboard!

Super Hawk: Semi-retired superhero alter ego of Fischer King. Adopted Rachel King (the Red Kite) when she was very young and abandoned her at a circus to "season" her. Kind of a jerk.

The Thinker: 10th-level conjurer with the ability to think objects into existence.

Treasure Chest: A would-be hero with a pocket dimension that occupies the area right above her heart. She never knows what the pocket dimension is going to provide for her. Real name...unknown! Well, she knows it.

Troll King (1): The lives-under-a-bridge-and-chews-on-your-bones kind.

Troll King (2): The internet kind. Fellow student at Van Buren. A jerk (as you'd expect with that name). 3rd-level computer griefer.

U.S. Ape: Patriotic soldier of fortune (and ape). Lt. Col. Retired. After the death of his wife and child, he moved underground (he makes his residence where no one will think to look for him: at the WB-Z).

Van Buren Middle School: Wilksboro's high security middle school.

Vanman: Part man, part van machine!

WB: Abbreviation for Wilksboro.

Wilksboro: Angel City's most dangerous neighborhood. If something earth-shakingly bad happens, it probably starts here. Abbreves to "WB".

WB-Z: Wilksboro's high security zoo. Only the meanest, craziest animals allowed. A dumping ground, of sorts, for the rest of the world's zoos. Also houses whatever can be caught in or strays from the Forbidden Zone (that can be caught or caged conventionally).

The Young Vandal

#streetangelfanart

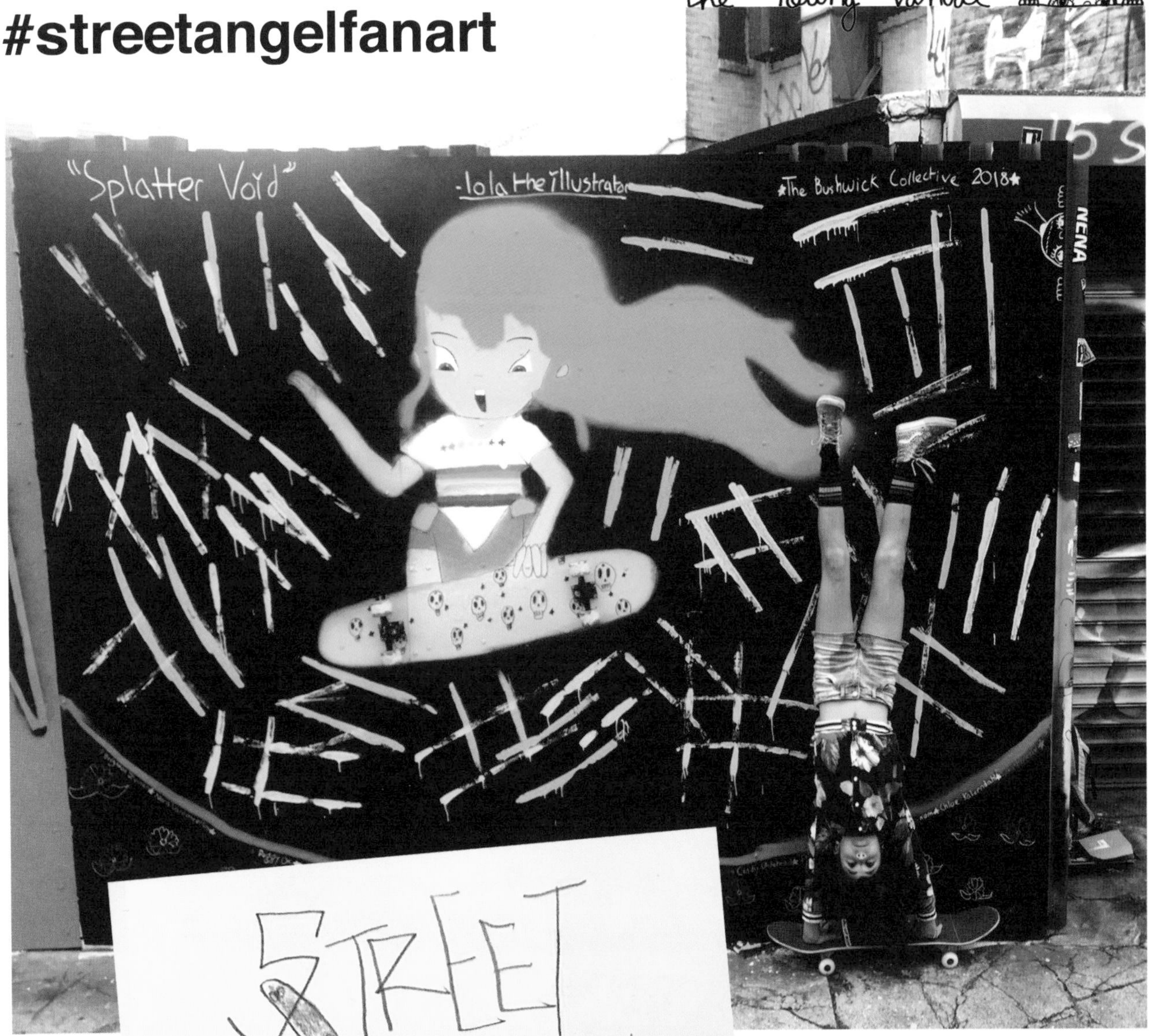
"Splatter Void"
-lola the illustrator
★The Bushwick Collective 2018★

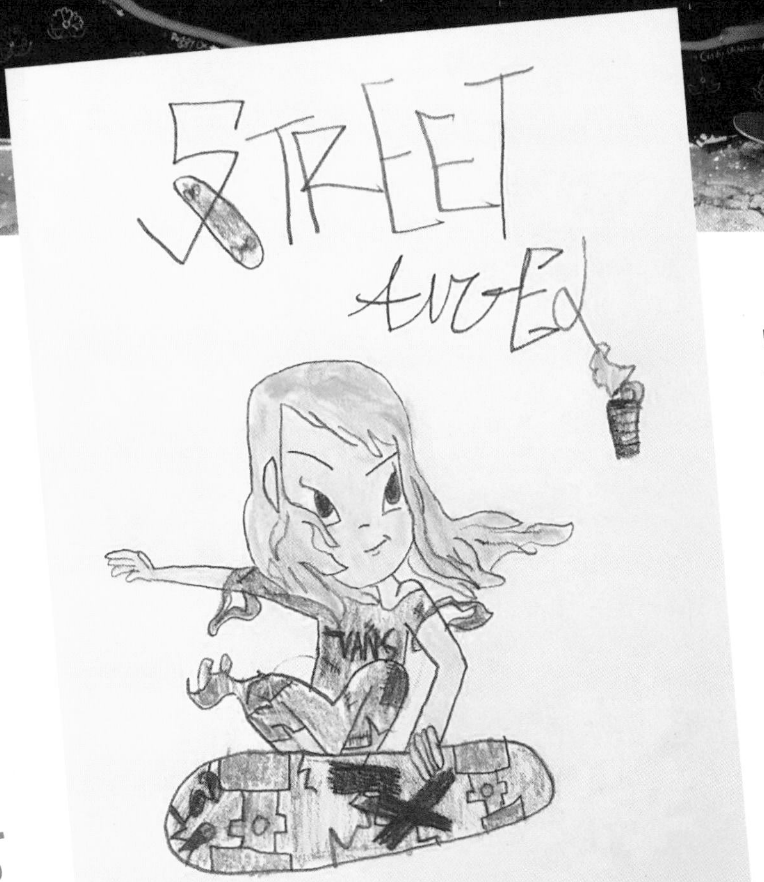
STREET
ANGEL
VANS
-lolatheillustrator

theyoungvandal.com

Lola the Illustrator started drawing at three and vandalizing walls when she was six years old. In 2014, she was caught creating some unauthorized street art in Bushwick, Brooklyn by Joe Ficalora, founder of the Bushwick Collective, who, after some initial scolding, invited her to join the team. Some of her influences include Jerkface, Magali Le Huche, Sipros, Dasic Fernández, Kylab, Chor Boogie, London Kaye, FKDL, Danielle Mastrion, and Hayao Miyazaki. When not painting or going to school, Lola enjoys reading (tons), writing stories and comics (also tons), skateboarding, and playing Nintendo games.

@lolatheillustrator

DUSTERS STREET ANGEL GN4LW CRUISER SKATEBOARD

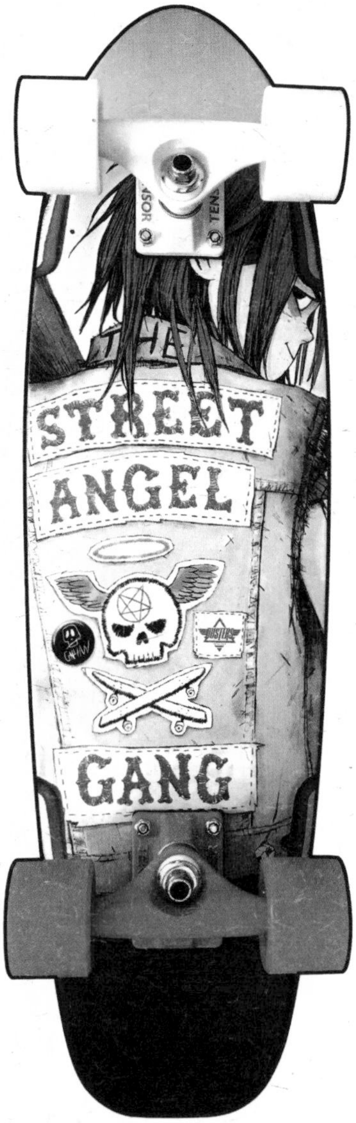
STREET
ANGEL
GANG

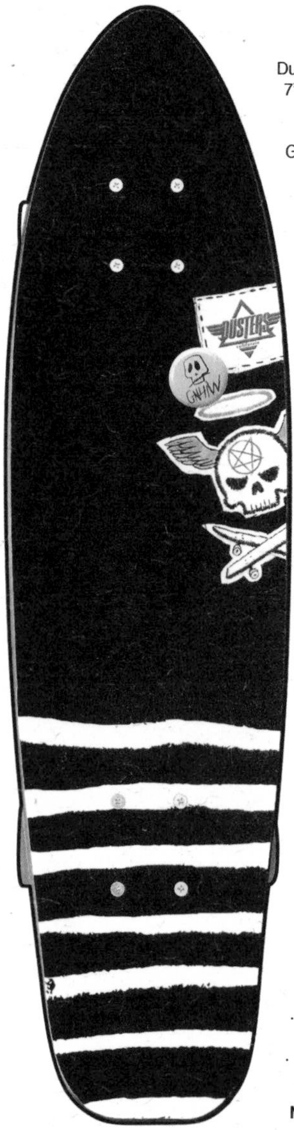
DUSTERS

Dusters Street Angel GN4LW
7"x25" Cruiser Skateboard

White / Pink -
Girl Is NOT a 4 Letter Word

Width: 7" / Length: 25" /
Wheelbase: 12.25"

Features:

- Collaboration with Girl is NOT a 4 Letter Word (girlisnota4letterword.com)
- Art by Jim Rugg
- A portion of the proceeds go to Girl is Not a 4 Letter Word Micro Grant Program
- Custom printed grip
- Tensor 4.25" trucks
- Dusters Abec 7 bearings
- Extended wheel wells
- 59mm x 43mm 83A wheels

No. 1744 - $129.95

dusterscalifornia.com

girlisnota4letterword.com

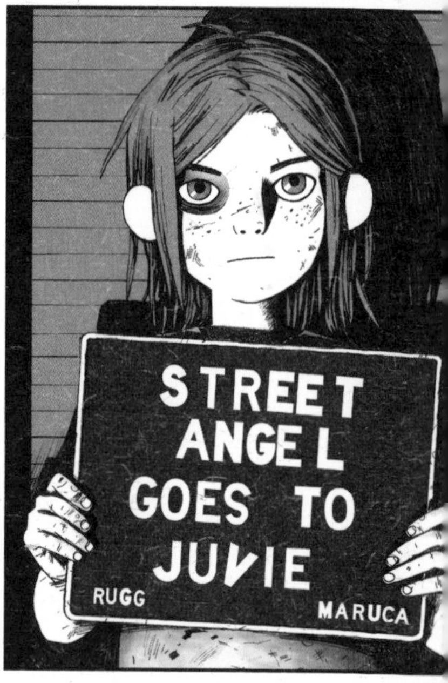
STREET
ANGEL
GOES TO
JUVIE
RUGG
MARUCA

STREET ANGEL: SUPER HERO FOR A DAY

Jesse knows the pressures of being the girl who always saves the day and she's okay with it. It's just who she is. But when she and her friends stumble across a powerful alien artifact - they soon realize that being a superhero isn't all fun and games.

Is this an alien plot to destroy their friendship or will Jess hock the artifact for a couple of hot dogs?

Story: Jim Rugg, Brian Maruca
Art / Cover: Jim Rugg
Hardcover: 48 pages
Publisher: Image Comics
ISBN-10: 153430553X
ISBN-13: 978-1534305533
Dimensions: 8.7 x 0.5 x 12.2 inches

No. 2244 - $19.99

STREET ANGEL PRINCESS OF POVERTY

Harry Potter, Bruce Wayne, Annie, and Oliver Twist can go #&©% themselves! There's a new orphan in town. Homeless teenager, Jesse "Street Angel" Sanchez cuts school and uses her skateboard and kung-fu action to fight ninja gangbangers, mad scientists, cops, time-traveling pirates, J-horror cliches, an evil version of her future self, ancient gods, rednecks, hunger...

Funny, violent, irreverent — everything you love in comic books!

Story/Art/Cover: Jim Rugg
Story: Brian Maruca
Hardcover: 196 pages
Publisher: AdHouse Books
ISBN-10: 1935233327
ISBN-13: 978-1935233329
Dimensions: 6.2 x 9 inches

No. 2027 - $19.95

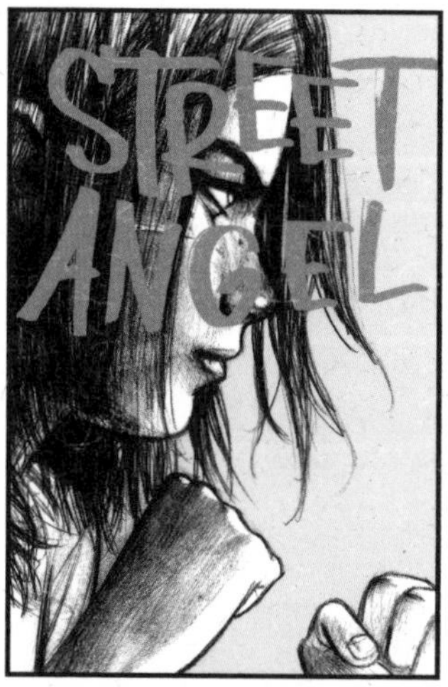
STREET
ANGEL

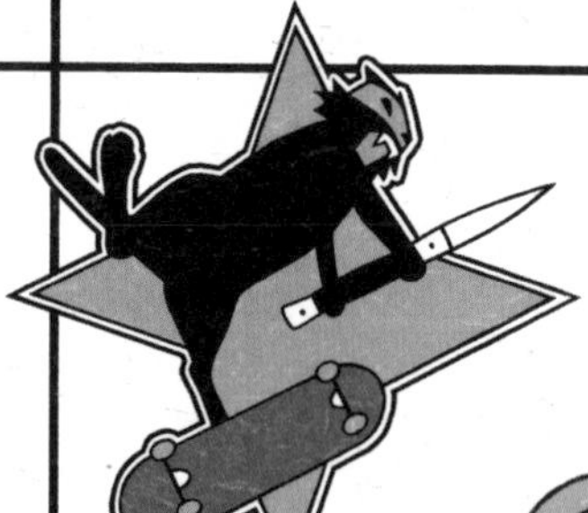

ENAMEL PINS

The perfec
finishing touch
for your stylish outfit

No. 111 - Ninja Cat
No. 112 - Street Angel
$9.95

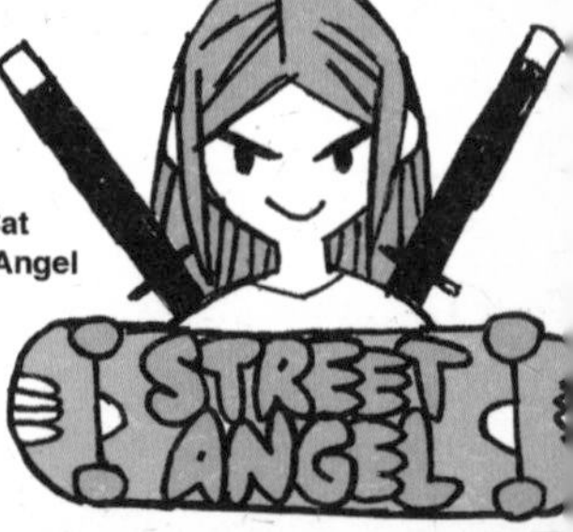
STREET
ANGEL

@jimruggart
jimrugg.com
jamesrugg@gmail.com

The Deadliest Girl